ILLUMINATION PRESENTS
Dr. Seuss'
The
GRINCH

The Deluxe Junior Novelization

Adapted by David Lewman

Based on the screenplay written by

Tommy Swedlow & Michael LeSieur

and based on Dr. Seuss characters

owned and licensed by

Dr. Seuss Enterprises, L.P.

Random House 🏠 New York

Published in the United States by Random House Children's Books,
a division of Penguin Random House LLC, 1745 Broadway, New York, NY 10019,
and in Canada by Penguin Random House Canada Limited, Toronto.
Random House and the colophon are registered trademarks
of Penguin Random House LLC.
rhcbooks.com
ISBN 978-0-525-58056-0 (hardcover)
ISBN 978-0-525-64451-4 (ebook)
Printed in the United States of America
10 9 8 7 6 5 4 3 2 1

1

Far past any place you've ever been, surrounded by snowy mountains and deep forests, was a beautiful, wonderful town like no other you've ever seen.

Who-ville!

Every day of the year, *Who*-ville was a happy, friendly town full of happy, friendly *Whos*. But there was one time of year when *Who*-ville became an even happier place, with festive holiday decorations and music all over town. In the weeks before Christmas, the *Whos* rushed around *Who*-ville buying presents, gift-wrapping paper, and delicious

food for their family feasts. On street corners, *Whos* handed out green wreaths and striped candy canes.

White sparkling snow fell on *Who*-ville in the wintertime, and the *Whos* loved it! They skied. They sledded. They skated. They made snowmen. A special machine even cranked out snowballs by the dozens for snowball fights.

Yes, the *Whos* down in *Who*-ville liked Christmas a lot.

But the Grinch, in his cave north of *Who*-ville, did NOT!

To get to the Grinch's cave, you had to head north out of *Who*-ville and up Mt. Crumpit past signs that read:

The Grinch did NOT like visitors.

Eventually the trail led through twisted iron gates to a door carved into the side of the mountain. Through that door, in a well-furnished cave with lots of rooms and chambers, lived the furry green Grinch and his faithful little dog, Max.

One winter, on a morning late in December,

the Grinch lay in bed under a pile of thick blankets, snoring. On his dresser across the room, the Grinch's big clock radio clicked from 6:59 to 7:00. The radio began to play a jolly Christmas song.

The Grinch's eyes popped open. Groaning, he stretched his furry green hand out from underneath the blankets and found a stack of books on his nightstand. He picked one up (*Spelunking for Beginners*) and tossed it at the clock radio. *WHOMP!*

But the book didn't turn the radio off. It just changed the station. A different, even jollier Christmas tune was playing.

The Grinch threw a tennis racquet at the radio. *WHACK!* The station changed to one playing yet another Christmas song.

Finally the Grinch threw a lamp at the clock radio, knocking it into a deep crevasse. The Grinch smiled and gave a satisfied little "Humph." But then he heard the radio echoing up from the rocky depths, still playing.

The Grinch sighed and called out, "MAX!" He yanked a rope that rang bells set up throughout the large cave. *DING-A-LING-A-LING!*

The bells woke Max right away. He jumped up from his little mattress and blue blanket, his eyes wide open and his brown tail wagging. He was ready for a new day! Max got right to work making his grouchy master (and best friend) a hot cup of coffee.

Up in his bedroom, the Grinch slowly emerged from the covers and sat up.

The cave was full of pulleys and levers to help Max do all his household chores. Max ran up a series of stairs and jumped onto a small platform, pushing the plunger down into a coffee pot, filling a cup. Pouring from a small measuring cup gripped tightly between his teeth, Max used steamed milk to draw a frowny face on top of the Grinch's coffee.

Max put the cup of coffee on a tray, carefully balanced the tray on his head, and backed into a mini-elevator. He pulled down on a handle, and a creaky elevator slowly carried him up to the Grinch's bedroom.

DING! The mini-elevator arrived inside the Grinch's nightstand. The door swung open and Max stepped out, careful not to spill a single drop of the hot coffee. Groaning and grunting, the Grinch took

the coffee. Clutching the cup, he stood up and slid his feet into his slippers. He slowly walked to the bathroom. He could still hear Christmas songs playing from the depths of the dark crevasse. He made a disgusted face.

"A shower's just the thing to drown out that racket," he growled.

The Grinch lingered awhile in the hot shower, scrubbing his green fur. When he stepped out of the shower, a blow-dryer turned on automatically, fluffing him up. Then he walked through an opening shaped like his body. The opening was lined with bristles to brush his fur and smooth it down.

Meanwhile, Max scurried into the Grinch's closet to fetch his master's outfit for the day. Using his mouth, he tugged the cord to turn on the closet light. Then he flipped through all the pairs of green pants hanging on labeled hangers. The labels read:

> BAD DAY
>
> DISGRUNTLED
>
> GRUMPY
>
> MISERABLE
>
> VERY MISERABLE

Max considered his master's current mood. With Christmas so near, the choice was obvious: VERY MISERABLE. Max pulled the hanger and the pants off the rod and handed them to the Grinch, who snapped the green pants on. *SNAP!*

Looking into the mirror again, the Grinch used a finger to swirl up the curly tuft of green fur on the top of his head, saying, "Boop!" He looked down and swirled Max's tuft up, too. "Boop!" Max wagged his tail. Their hair was perfect now.

The Grinch crossed his bedroom and plopped down into a big red chair under an opening in the ceiling. His weight triggered a spring that lifted the chair up through the hole and into the dining room. He arrived right at his place at the table.

Max, who had already hurried up to the dining room, yanked a rope. The rope snaked through a system of pulleys that lifted the round cover off the Grinch's plate.

"Ooh, I am starving!" the Grinch said, leaning forward to see what delicious dish Max had prepared for his breakfast. He blinked.

Sitting on the plate was a single bean.

2

Baffled by the meager breakfast, the Grinch turned to Max for an explanation. "What is this?"

"Arf! Arf! Arf!" Max barked.

"No, no, no, no," the Grinch disagreed, shaking his head. "That's impossible! We can't be out of food!"

He ran to the kitchen. Every cabinet he flung open was empty. "Where's my personal reserve of Moose Juice and Goose Juice?" he cried. "My emergency stash of *Who* Hash? And my secret slew of frozen Beezle-Nut Stew?"

The Grinch stared at the empty shelves. "I specifically bought enough food to last until January!" He patted his stomach. "How much *emotional eating* have I been doing?"

The cabinet containing Max's dog food was also empty. The loyal—and very hungry—Max stared at the Grinch with his big eyes, as if to say, "You know what you have to do."

The Grinch held up his hands, protesting, "No, I won't. I will not." He folded his arms across his chest stubbornly. "I am not going to *Who*-ville during Chrrr . . ." He struggled to spit out the word he hated so much. "Chrisss . . . argh. Chrrriii . . . Christmas! Ugh!"

Max nudged his empty food bowl toward the Grinch.

"Fine," he said, giving in to the unavoidable. "But I'm going to despise every second of it."

Yes, the Grinch HATED Christmas! No one knew why, but some suspected it was because his heart was two sizes too small. And the last thing he wanted

to do was go into *Who*-ville at Christmastime.

As the wind howled and sleet blew, the Grinch and Max trudged through the twisted iron gates and headed down Mt. Crumpit into *Who*-ville. The Grinch wore a long red-and-white-striped scarf around his neck.

In *Who*-ville, it was a busy, bustling early morning. Looking as though it had been built out of gingerbread, the whole town was covered in Christmas decorations. Every store window, every streetlamp, and every bench was decked out with garlands and tinsel. The place positively glowed with good cheer and excitement.

A bus pulled up to a bus stop. The driver leaned out and greeted one of the waiting *Whos*. "Hey, Ted!" the driver called out in a friendly voice.

"Morning!" Ted said as he climbed aboard. Other passengers behind him said their cheerful good mornings. The driver closed the doors and pulled away from the snowy curb. *VROOM!*

Down the street, Donna *Who* ran to catch the

bus. "Wait!" she shouted. "Wait, hold the bus!" She dodged other *Whos* on the crowded sidewalk as she ran. "Excuse me. Sorry. Coming through!"

By running as fast as she could, Donna managed to catch up with the bus and run alongside it. "Wait!" she yelled again. "Wait! Sam, hold the bus!"

Sam, the driver, heard Donna yelling outside. "Oh!" he said when he saw her. He stopped the bus right away and opened the doors.

"Oof!" Donna grunted as she fell in the snow. She picked herself up and climbed the steps, brushing snow off her coat and pants.

"Sorry, Donna," the driver apologized.

"That's okay, Sam," she replied, panting. "Thanks for stopping! Whew!"

Under her winter coat, Donna had on the medical scrubs she wore for her job as a nurse. She dug out coins and dropped them into the fare box. *DING! DING! DING!*

"They still got you on the night shift, huh?" Sam asked.

"Sure do." Donna nodded.

"Oh, by the way," Sam said, "Cindy-Lou forgot her hockey stick."

"Of course she did," Donna said, smiling. "That's my girl." Sometimes Donna thought her daughter would forget her own nose if it weren't attached to her face. Especially in the days just before Christmas.

As he and Max reached the edge of town, the Grinch sang to himself gloomily, "Jingle bells, Christmas smells, make it go away! Dee dee da, dee dee dee da . . ."

Trying to avoid all the holiday cheer, he hurried past the decorated stores and the *Whos* in their colorful sweaters. But four *Whos* singing Christmas carols spotted the elusive Grinch and followed him through the town, determined to serenade him.

The Grinch screamed and ran!

3

Breathing hard, the Grinch ducked into the town's general store. *DING!* A cheerful bell rang as the Grinch pushed the door open. A friendly *Who* clerk with a thick brown mustache smiled and greeted him. "Oh, hello! Happy holi—"

But the Grinch held up a finger to stop him. "Nuh-uh," he interrupted, cutting off the clerk's good Christmas wishes.

Moving down the aisles of the store, the Grinch scooped can after can of *Who* Hash into a little wagon Max was pulling. He turned the corner into

a new aisle and passed a shopper who was staring at the shelves of food. While the shopper wasn't looking, the Grinch snatched a jar of spicy pickles out of her basket, screwed off the lid, pulled out a pickle, and shoved the whole thing into his mouth. Then he made a disgusted face. "Blech."

He spat the pickle back into the jar, screwed the lid back on, and dropped the jar into another customer's basket! Neither of the shoppers noticed what the mean grouch had done.

He passed another shopper who was trying to reach a jar on a high shelf. She stood on her tiptoes, stretching her arms. The Grinch reached around her and plucked the jar off the shelf. "Eh, what's this?" he sniffed, reading the jar's label.

"Ooh!" the lady *Who* exclaimed. "Excuse me."

She tapped the Grinch on the shoulder. He turned to look at her and drew back, wanting nothing to do with any of the *Whos*. The lady pointed at the jar. "Are you getting that?" she asked. "I need it for my Christmas stuffing."

"Hmm," mused the Grinch, looking at her. "No." Smiling, he put the jar back on the high shelf where

the lady couldn't possibly reach it. Then he walked away.

"Well!" said the lady, shocked by his unbelievably rude behavior. "That's not very nice."

Before he reached the end of the aisle, the Grinch gave the shelf a sharp bump with his elbow. The jar tottered, tipped, fell, and shattered on the floor. *CRASH!*

"Oh, sugarplum," the lady *Who* said.

The Grinch chuckled a nasty chuckle as he walked away.

In her kitchen, Donna stood by the sink, trying her best to unclog it with a toy arrow. She held a telephone between her ear and her shoulder as she struggled with the clogged sink.

"I just got off the night shift," she told her friend on the other end of the line. "I have a list of errands a mile long, AND the babysitter left the kitchen sink clogged up."

Donna said goodbye and called to her daughter, "Cindy-Lou, sweetheart, come eat!"

"Coming!" Cindy-Lou answered.

Donna stopped trying to unclog the sink and turned to the stove to take the teakettle off the burner. The water had come to a boil, so the kettle was whistling loudly. *TWWEEEEE!* "All right," Donna said to the kettle. She set it on a cool burner. As she opened a bag of bread, she noticed her son Buster teething on his twin brother, Bean's, head. "Buster, we've talked about this," she reminded him. "Your brother's head is not breakfast."

She tossed a couple of bread slices in the toaster and pushed down the handle. After that she poured cereal into bowls and set them in front of her twin boys. At the sight of the cereal, they turned up their noses. "Blech!" Buster said, sticking his tongue out.

Exhausted, Donna slumped over the sink for a moment. Her daughter, Cindy-Lou, popped through the door, bundled up for the cold weather. Her blond hair was braided into two long pigtails tied in bows. She had blue eyes and a big smile, and almost everything she wore was pink. She held an envelope. "You all right, Mom?" she asked when she saw her mother.

Donna forced a smile and turned to face Cindy-Lou. "Yes! Never better!" She pointed to the sink. "What'd you put down here, anyway? A roller skate?"

"No," Cindy-Lou answered. "Just batter. Me and Mrs. Wilbur made cookies."

"Oh, that explains it," Donna said. "Come have some eggs."

"I can't," Cindy-Lou said, shaking her head. "I gotta go mail something. But I made the beds and put away the twins' toys."

"Thanks, sweetheart," Donna said, smiling. "You didn't have to do that."

Cindy-Lou shrugged. She liked helping her mom. "I don't mind." She sniffed the air. "Something's burning."

"Just a second, sweetie," Donna said, turning her attention to the twins. "Bean, don't feed your brother with your feet." Bean had his foot in Buster's mouth.

"Mom, the toast!" Cindy-Lou cried, seeing black smoke rising from the toaster.

"I got it!" Donna said, hurrying over to the toaster. She popped the singed slices out, put them on plates, and set them in front of the twins. The

boys grabbed the toast and happily chomped away.

"I'll be back soon, Mom!" Cindy-Lou said, turning to leave.

"Wait," Donna said. "Where are you going, again?"

"I told you," Cindy-Lou said, energetically waving the envelope. "To mail a letter."

"Okay, but just come here first," Donna said, stretching out her arms.

"Mom, I gotta go," Cindy-Lou insisted. Then she relented. "All right," she sighed. She went to her mom, who hugged her and kissed her forehead.

"Okay," Donna said. "Now you can go."

Cindy-Lou hurried out, saying, "Thanks, Mom! Bye, Buster! Bye, Bean!"

"Don't do anything I wouldn't do!" Donna called after her.

"Roger that, Mom!" Cindy-Lou said as she went out the door.

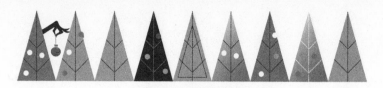

4

Outside, Cindy-Lou tossed her inflatable pink snow tube down on the ground, jumped on it, and zipped downhill. "Wooo!" she whooped as her snow tube picked up speed. "Here goes Cindy-Lou *Who*," she said, trying to sound like a sports announcer, "as she dashes through the snow with a very important letter!"

Down at the base of the hill, several blocks away, the mail carrier drove his dogsled toward a mailbox to pick up its cards, letters, and packages. "Oh no!"

Cindy-Lou cried when she spotted him. "I'm going to miss the mailman!"

She realized that if she continued on her current path, the mail carrier would be long gone by the time she reached the mailbox. "Shortcut!" she said, making a quick decision. She leaned forward on her snow tube and made a sharp turn. "Go, go, go, go!"

Cindy-Lou blasted through the blowing snow, zipping along on her snow tube, leaning as far forward as she dared. She didn't want to fall off, especially at the speed she was going. *WHOOSH!* She hit a small hill that launched her into the air! "Whoooaaah!" she yelled.

WHUMP! Cindy-Lou landed on the roof of a house, slid across it, and bounced onto the roof of the next house! Spinning and twirling, she was going faster and faster. "Whoa, whoa, whoa!" she shouted, feeling a little out of control, but enjoying the speed.

WHOMP! She hit the ground and kept sliding, going right through the open front door of a house. "Oh boy," she muttered. At this point, she was going so fast that she didn't even need to be on the snow

anymore. She slid right through the dining room, where a family of *Whos* were finishing up their breakfast.

"Bon appétit!" she said cheerfully to the surprised *Whos* as she headed on out the back door. In their backyard, she hit another small sloping incline, which sent her flying into the air. "Woo-hoo!" she whooped.

A gust of wind snatched the envelope out of her hand. "Oh no!" she cried, watching it blow away. There was no way for her to turn around to retrieve her letter. In fact, she couldn't even stop! Her snow tube didn't have any brakes. She just kept zooming through *Who*-ville, picking up even more speed. "Whoooaah!" Cindy-Lou screamed. "Aaaaaaah!" She looked around, trying to spot the fluttering envelope as it was carried by the winter wind. Occasionally she'd see it, heading in the same direction as she was. Maybe she could find it once it landed on the snow. If only she could stop!

Near the mailbox, the Grinch and Max crossed the street with their wagon full of groceries. Looking down on the pair, Cindy-Lou saw that she was going

to run right into them! "Watch out!" she warned.

The Grinch looked up with alarm and saw a little girl on an inflatable snow tube flying straight toward Max and him! "Ahhh!" he yelled as she plummeted out of the sky.

WHAM! Cindy-Lou crashed into the Grinch, knocking him into a snowbank! "Ooof!" the Grinch grunted. "Gaah. Uggh!"

He raised his head and spat snow out of his mouth. "PTOOO!"

Cindy-Lou crawled around on all fours, frantically searching the snow for her missing envelope. "No!" she cried. "My letter!"

The Grinch slowly got back to his feet. "What is wrong with you?!" he demanded. "Didn't you see me?!" He pulled at the pink snow tube that had somehow gotten wrapped around his body in the collision. "I mean, if this thing were a sled, I'd . . . I'd . . . well, I'd be a goner!"

Cindy-Lou stopped searching for her letter and looked at the Grinch as he freed himself from the snow tube. "I'm sorry for bumping into you, but this is really important. Have you seen my letter? It's in

an envelope. And it would have come falling down out of the sky. After I dropped it."

She resumed searching the snowy ground around them. Looking disgusted, the Grinch turned to Max and said, "And that right there is the true nature of the *Who* child. Always going straight back to 'me, me, me, my letter, me, me, me.'"

Cindy-Lou shook her head. "No," she insisted, "you don't understand. This isn't just a letter. This is *the* letter!"

Her explanation failed to impress the Grinch.

"Oh, really," he said sarcastically. "Let me guess." He looked Cindy-Lou up and down, as if he was searching for clues. "Small child. On December 20. Rabidly searching for a 'really important' lost letter." He stroked his chin and looked up to the sky, pretending to think. "Might this letter contain your list of greedy demands to Santa?"

Cindy-Lou stood up, offended. She pulled herself up to her full height and looked the Grinch in the eye. "First of all," she said firmly, "I'm not that small. And second of all, they're not demands. It's

more like a wish, and what I'm wishing for is really, really important!"

Raising his eyebrows, the Grinch pretended to care. "Well, then why send a letter?" he asked sarcastically. "I mean, if it's really that important, you should just ask Santa face to face!" He pretended to remember something. "Oh, but that's right—no one's ever seen him. My bad." He turned to his dog. "Come on, Max. Let's get out of here."

As the Grinch and Max walked off, Cindy-Lou watched them go. "Bye, doggy," she said to Max, who wagged his tail.

The letter floated down out of the sky and landed at Cindy-Lou's feet. She stared at it, thinking about what the Grinch had said.

5

As they made their way through *Who*-ville, heading back to Mt. Crumpit, the Grinch and Max passed the home of a bushy-bearded *Who* named Bricklebaum. Wearing a green hat and a red sweater with green Christmas trees on it, Bricklebaum was putting lots and lots of decorations on his house. As he worked, he sang the random words to different Christmas carols: "Hum-de-dum-dum Christmas . . . dah-de-dah-dah . . . mistletoe . . . It's de dum dum dum dum dum. . . ."

"Whoa!" the Grinch said when he spotted his

neighbor. "There he is, Max!" he said in a low voice so Bricklebaum wouldn't hear. "The happiest *Who* alive, the unbearable Bricklebaum!" Out of the side of his mouth, he told Max, "He thinks we're friends."

The Grinch ducked out of sight, hoping to avoid the cheerful *Who*. He peered around a tree, watching Bricklebaum putting up what seemed to be miles of Christmas lights. The Grinch found the whole gaudy spectacle disgusting.

"Have a la-la-la-la Christmas," Bricklebaum kept singing loudly. "It's de dum dum dum dum dum. . . ."

The Grinch decided Bricklebaum was too busy to notice them passing by. "He's not looking," he said to Max. "Quick, let's make a run for it!"

Still singing, Bricklebaum climbed a ladder to the roof of his house. The roof was covered with lights, candy canes, and an impressively giant Santa's sleigh complete with eight plastic reindeer. He'd strung even more lights along the gutters, running all the electrical cords to a master switch. Cords also led to inflatable Christmas characters down in the yard: a penguin, a Santa Claus, giant presents, a teddy bear, and others.

The Grinch pressed up against the tree that he and Max were hiding behind. "Go, go, go, go, go!" he hissed to Max.

"What?" Bricklebaum said, looking around. He thought he'd heard something. "What was that?" But he didn't see anyone. "No," he said to himself, shaking his head. He resumed singing, ". . . say hello and mistletoe and ho ho ho!"

As Bricklebaum turned back to his work, hitting a button to inflate all the decorations, the Grinch and Max made a mad dash for it. The Grinch wove between the big inflatable figures while Max followed with the cart full of groceries. They were almost clear when—

WHAP! An inflatable snowman rose up, filling with air. Its arm sprang out and smacked the Grinch in the face, knocking him right into the wagon of groceries. He ended up sprawled facedown in the snow. "Augh! Oof!"

"Oh my goodness, Mr. Grinch!" he cried. "I'm coming!" He scrambled down his ladder.

The Grinch lifted his head and shook snow off his face. He got up and started testily gathering his

scattered groceries as fast as he could, hoping to escape before the friendly *Who* arrived to help. Bricklebaum rushed past the inflatable snowman, telling it, "Leave Mr. Grinch alone!" When he reached the Grinch, Bricklebaum said, "That's one tough balloon that you're fighting there. Here, come on. Let me help you."

"I do not want or need your help," the Grinch protested.

But Bricklebaum began brightly picking up groceries and setting them back on the overloaded little wagon. He paused, looking at one item. "Oh, hair dye?" he said, laughing as he read the label. "Gorgeous Green Goddess!"

"Oh!" the Grinch exclaimed, snatching the hair dye out of Bricklebaum's hand.

Bricklebaum could see the Grinch was embarrassed. "Hey, I'm sorry if I made you uncomfy," he said. "We all gotta keep the gray away. I myself use 'Chocolate Explosion.'"

"You know what?" the Grinch interrupted as he buried the hair dye at the bottom of the wagon. "If you want to apologize, apologize for THAT!" He

pointed an accusing green finger at Bricklebaum's overly decorated house. "You're a grown man with a life-size Santa's sleigh on your roof!"

"Don't blame me!" Bricklebaum said. "Haven't you heard? The mayor of *Who*-ville wants Christmas to be three times bigger this year! That means three times the lights! Three times the eggnog! Three times the—"

"—information needed," the Grinch said, sarcastically finishing Bricklebaum's sentence for him.

Bricklebaum just laughed. "Ha ha! That's a good one!" It seemed as though nothing could spoil the happy *Who*'s good mood. Not even the Grinch's sarcasm.

He handed the Grinch a flyer. It told all about how this was going to be the biggest Christmas they had ever seen. The Grinch studied the pamphlet, then broke into laughter. "Oh, I get it!" he said. "This is one of your 'kidding' things! Finally! Something you said is actually funny!"

Bricklebaum laughed, too. "Yeah, I do kid a lot," he agreed. "But, no, this is actually—"

"Christmas three times bigger!" the Grinch said, laughing.

"Look," Bricklebaum said, pointing at the flyer. "It says right there that—"

"It's hysterical!" the Grinch cried, helpless with laughter. "Oh, dear! Ohhhh, no, no, no."

"Well, you're just going to have a good time with this, aren't you?" Bricklebaum observed. "I gotta say, it's really nice to see you laughing."

"Sorry, I can't hear you," the Grinch said, still laughing. "I don't speak ridiculous. Oh, you're a scream. Have a nice life. Goodbye!"

He stomped away through the snow with Max pulling the wagon. They headed up the hill toward Mt. Crumpit.

"I'll see you later!" Bricklebaum called after them, waving.

The Grinch and Max made their way up the mountain. Partway up, the Grinch dropped Bricklebaum's flyer and stepped on it.

6

That night, bright Christmas lights came on all over *Who*-ville. Inside Cindy-Lou *Who*'s house, Donna was decorating the tree with help from the twins, Bean and Buster. Bean moved toward the tree, holding a shiny ornament.

"Yup, that's right," Donna said encouragingly. "That's a great spot. Right there."

Bean turned and tried to hang the ornament on Buster's ear.

"No, no, not on your brother," Donna said, hurrying to take the ornament from Bean, who was

delighted with his handiwork. "Let Mommy do it."

From the top of the stairs, Cindy-Lou looked down at her mom and her brothers through thick snow goggles. She was so bundled up in coats and scarves and gloves and boots, she could barely move. She took one step . . .

. . . and tumbled down the stairs! "Whoa!" she yelled as she rolled down. *THUMP THUMP THUMP THUMP THUMP!*

"Cindy-Lou!" Donna cried, rushing to her daughter's side at the bottom of the stairs. "Are you all right?"

"Yeah," Cindy-Lou said, lying there, staring up at the ceiling. "I'm okay."

"You scared me," Donna said.

Despite all the clothing and gear she was wearing, Cindy-Lou managed to struggle back up onto her feet. "Don't worry, Mom," she said. "I'm wearing four ski jackets. Broke my fall."

"Four jackets?" Donna asked. "Aren't you a little hot?"

"Yep," Cindy-Lou admitted with enthusiastic good cheer. "Sweatin' a little bit."

Donna took a good look at her daughter, dressed for a blizzard, a hurricane, and an ice storm all rolled into one. "Are you going somewhere?"

"North Pole," Cindy-Lou answered, pulling a zipper up to her chin.

"Oh, wow!" Donna said. "Any particular reason?"

Cindy-Lou nodded. "I gotta talk to Santa."

Donna walked back to the box of Christmas decorations and picked up another ornament. "Santa, huh?"

"Yeah," her daughter said. "It's real important."

"Well, it must be if you need to go see him in person," Donna agreed.

Cindy-Lou grabbed her hockey stick and waddled toward the door. "Yup, it sure is."

"Okay, then," Donna said, hanging the ornament on the tree. "Well, good luck and I'll see you in about a month."

Cindy-Lou stopped in her tracks. "Wait. It takes a whole month to get to the North Pole?"

"Oh yeah," Donna said, reaching in the box for another ornament. "At least."

Cindy-Lou stood by the door, thinking.

"Christmas would be over by the time I got there."

"That's true!" Donna said, as though she hadn't thought of that. "Yeah, we would miss you at Christmas."

"Wow," Cindy-Lou said, shaking her head. "I guess I'm going to have to come up with another plan."

Donna hung the ornament on the tree, dug through the box, and pulled out a plastic halo. "Hey, maybe while you're thinking, you could put the halo on the angel," she suggested.

"Okay," Cindy-Lou said.

Donna put her hands on her daughter's shoulders and carefully guided her toward the tree. She didn't want her to trip and fall right into it. "You want to take your jackets off?"

"Yeah, at least one or two of them," Cindy-Lou said, laughing. Donna laughed, too. She handed the halo to her daughter and looked around for the angel. She spotted it.

"No, boys, don't pull the angel's wings off," Donna said, hurrying to stop the twins' latest endeavor. "She needs those."

At the same moment that Cindy-Lou was deciding not to go to the North Pole to see Santa, the Grinch was standing outside his cave, staring down at *Who*-ville from his chilly perch on Mt. Crumpit. He wasn't decorating a tree that night. And he certainly had no plans to go see Santa.

He turned away from the twinkling lights of *Who*-ville and went back inside his cave. He sat down in his big red chair by the fireplace. He thought about the *Whos*, all snug in their homes together, and then he thought about himself, sitting all alone.

"It is better this way," he told himself, staring into the crackling fire.

7

At seven the next morning, the Grinch's clock radio dutifully turned on even though it was at the bottom of a crevasse surrounded by other thrown and broken objects. A jaunty holiday tune echoed up into the Grinch's bedroom. He woke up, realized what he was hearing, and gave a loud, frustrated groan. He grabbed a handy chair and hurled it into the darkness, where it smashed down onto the clock radio. The radio went silent.

"Heh heh," chuckled the Grinch, satisfied.

After his morning shower, the Grinch made his

way up to the dining room and sat at one end of a long wooden table. Max sat at the other. They ate their breakfast in silence.

"So," the Grinch said when he'd finished eating, "what do you want to do today?"

Max thought about it.

A little while later, the Grinch sat hunched over the keyboard of his massive pipe organ, dramatically playing a slow, sad melody. Playing a makeshift drum set, Max did his best to liven up the music with snappy snare hits and cymbal crashes. But every time he played some happy rhythms on the drums, the Grinch scowled at him.

Soon the Grinch came to the end of the gloomy piece of music. Max added a long, snappy solo on the cymbals. Annoyed, the Grinch pointed, ordering Max to leave.

Max slid off his stool and started to go, but then turned back and gave the biggest cymbal one more whack. *CLANG!*

Going straight to the kitchen, Max lay down and sadly curled up in a ball. Moments later, the Grinch popped up through the floor in his mechanical chair.

Seeing Max moping, he felt bad. "All right, all right, I'm sorry," he apologized. "You're a good dog but a bad drummer. What would you like to do?"

Max sat up and wagged his tail. He had an idea!

In the cave's study, which was lined with bookshelves, Max and the Grinch sat in big chairs, playing a game of chess. The Grinch stared down at the board, stuck. He couldn't see a move that didn't end with him losing. "More than embarrassing to be beaten by a dog," he muttered to himself under his breath.

He grabbed a squeaky ball beneath the table, squeezed it *(SQUEAK SQUEAK)*, and tossed it. "Oh, what's that?" he said innocently.

While Max rushed off to investigate, the green cheater quickly rearranged the pieces on the chessboard. "And checkmate!" the Grinch loudly and triumphantly announced. "Again!"

Suddenly, the whole room started to shake! Pieces fell off the board! Books tumbled off the shelves onto the floor. "What in the world is happening?" the Grinch cried.

He ran out of the study, hurrying to his front

door. He flung it open and went outside to see if he could figure out what was causing the shaking. An earthquake? Rockslide? Avalanche of snow?

Then he looked to the left and saw the biggest Christmas tree he'd ever seen. It was held aloft by several large hot-air balloons. The Grinch's jaw dropped at the sheer size of the tree. Pine needles rained down on the Grinch and Max. "What is that?" the Grinch cried.

"It's the most beautiful Christmas tree you've ever seen!" a familiar voice answered.

The Grinch scowled. Bricklebaum.

He was helping guide the giant tree down the mountain to *Who*-ville, where it would be set up in the town square.

Staring at the huge tree, the Grinch said to himself, "Three times bigger?" Then he screamed up to Bricklebaum, "That's a hundred times bigger!"

"Oh, you just wait until we light it tonight!" Bricklebaum enthused. "It'll sparkle so bright, you'll be celebrating Christmas with the rest of us! Ha ha! Oh, I can't wait! All we have to do is get it safely down the mountain! I'll see you later, Grinchy!"

"No, you will not see me later!" the Grinch insisted. "And I will not be celebrating! And that tree . . . that tree . . . has GOT TO GO!"

The Grinch turned on his heel and went back into his cave, slamming the door behind him. *WHAM!*

That night the festive streets of *Who*-ville were full of excited *Whos* making their way to the town square for the lighting of the tremendous Christmas tree. They all carried ornaments to hang on the tree's branches. It was like a parade of ornaments!

Cindy-Lou, Donna, Bean, and Buster carried the biggest ornaments they could find. As the family hurried toward the square, they admired their neighbors' colorful ornaments, which came in every shape and size.

"Come on, Mom!" Cindy-Lou shouted. She wanted to make sure their ornaments got good spots on the tree.

Cindy-Lou and her family reached the town square, where Mayor McGerkle was already onstage.

"Oh, how marvelous this time of year is!" he announced. "Welcome, citizens of *Who*-ville, to the annual tree-lighting ceremony! How spectacular are these ornaments?!"

Bricklebaum was carrying a big dragon ornament with a Santa beard and costume. "Look what I made, everybody! It's a Christmas dragon! It came to me in a dream!" Laughing merrily, he lifted the ornament for all to see.

Cindy-Lou handed her family's angel ornament to a *Who* in a crane's bucket that would rise to the top of the enormous tree. "Here you go!" Cindy-Lou said to the *Who*.

"Hey, Bartholomew!" Donna said to the *Who*.

"Hey there, Ms. *Who*," he answered cheerfully. "Nice angel!"

"Thank you!" Donna said. "Please find a good spot for it!"

Cindy-Lou watched as the bucket rose higher and higher. "There it goes," she said. Bartholomew carefully placed the angel on the tree.

"Of all the nights in the year," Mayor McGerkle was telling the crowd, "this is my favorite. Now let's

get ready to flip that switch and light up the sky!"

The *Whos,* excited and happy, circled around the base of the tree.

But up on Mt. Crumpit, watching the ceremony through a large pair of binoculars, the Grinch was not happy. He could tell that the mayor was about to flip the switch to turn on the tree's lights. "Oh, no," the Grinch said in a low voice. "Not on my watch, you don't."

8

Down by the tree, Cindy-Lou waved to her mom as she ran off. "See you guys soon! I'm going to go find Groopert," she explained. Groopert was Cindy-Lou's best friend.

"Okay, have fun! Bye!" Donna said. She turned to the twins. "Say 'bye!'" But the boys were too busy staring at all the ornaments on the tree to notice their mom or their sister as she made her way through the festive crowd.

Cindy-Lou quickly found Groopert. It was easy to spot her pal with the bright-red curly hair. Today

he was running a snowball stand. He handed a snow-ball to a young *Who*. "Here you go," Groopert said. "I hope your big brother gets what he deserves."

Cindy-Lou ran up, excited to see her friend. "Hey, Groopert! How's business?"

"Good," Groopert said, smiling. "What I can't sell"—he banged his fist down on the stand; a board swung down, changing the sign from SNOWBALLS! to SNOWCONES!—"I can always eat!" he said, pouring colorful syrup on a snowball. He took a big bite. Then he made a pained face.

"Aw, brain freeze!" he groaned.

"I need to talk to you about something really important," Cindy-Lou told him in a whisper. "Come on! Let's go!"

"Okay," Groopert said, rubbing his forehead. He banged his stand again, and a third board swung down with a sign that read NOW CLOSED! He and Cindy-Lou took off through the crowd.

Cindy-Lou and Groopert knew a good place for important talks. There was a carousel in *Who*-ville. In the center column of the carousel was a stair-case leading up to the top. The only person who

ever used the staircase was the maintenance *Who* in charge of keeping the carousel running smoothly. And like every other *Who* in *Who*-ville, he was at the tree-lighting ceremony.

Cindy-Lou climbed the stairs, her cautious footsteps echoing in the empty chamber. "All right, check this out, Groopert. I'm going to stay up on Christmas Eve this year and meet Santa Claus!"

Climbing the stairs behind her, Groopert was stunned by his friend's idea. "Whoa. That is crazy!"

Cindy-Lou stopped and turned around to face Groopert. "Yeah," she said. "I've really got to talk to him."

"About what?" Groopert asked.

She resumed climbing. They were almost to the top of the carousel. "Well," she said. "It's really personal, but I'm going to tell you because you're my best friend." They reached the top. From up there, they could see the crowd of *Whos* around the Christmas tree. "It's about my mom," Cindy-Lou continued. "All she ever does is work and take care of us, and it just isn't fair."

Cindy-Lou spotted her mom in the crowd,

holding Buster and Bean. "She acts like she's fine," Cindy-Lou said, "but I know it's really hard for her. I figured if anyone could fix that, it'd be Santa."

"Wow," Groopert said, impressed with his friend's generosity. "And I just asked for gum."

They heard Mayor McGerkle's voice saying, "Here we go!"

"It's starting!" Cindy-Lou cried.

"My favorite part of the night: the tree lighting!" the mayor said. "Okay, *Who*-ville, time to light this beautiful tree!"

But way, way up on Mt. Crumpit, the Grinch had other plans.

He paced along a rocky ledge, counting his steps through the snow. "Seventeen, eighteen, nineteen, and twenty!" Laughing, he set the brake on the wheel of a large homemade catapult! In its bucket sat a huge snowball, which the Grinch intended to launch right into the *Whos'* Christmas tree!

He hooked a long rope to the catapult. Then he attached the other end of the rope to a lever. When he yanked the rope, the catapult would fling the giant snowball at the tree and knock it over!

"Okay, locked and loaded," he said gleefully. Bending down on the edge of a cliff overlooking the town, he tightened the trigger rope.

Concentrating on the rope, the Grinch didn't notice when the brake on the catapult's wheel came loose. The catapult started rolling down the slope, straight toward him!

"ARF! ARF! ARF!" Max warned frantically.

"I know," the Grinch said without looking up. "I wish I could see the look on their faces when their beloved tree gets—"

WHAM! The catapult slammed into the Grinch, knocking him over the edge of the cliff! Holding desperately on to the catapult, the Grinch dangled over the steep drop. "Whoa!" he shouted. "Oh boy, oh boy, oh boy . . ."

The catapult started to tip over the cliff's edge. The Grinch managed to scramble up the catapult's beam, but the big snowball rolled out of the bucket and right toward him!

"WHOAAAHHH!" He dodged the snowball, which fell harmlessly into a deep ravine.

The Grinch climbed up the main beam of the

catapult and sat in the bucket. He sighed with relief. "Whew! That could have been so much worse—"

SNAP! The rope holding the bucket in place broke! *FWING!* The bucket flew forward!

"YAAAAAHHHHH!!!"

The Grinch was flung far into the air toward *Who*-ville!

9

Down in the town square, Mayor McGerkle stood near a large light switch at the base of the tree. "Let's begin the countdown!" he called out. "Ready, everyone? Count with me!"

Above, the Grinch sailed through the air, rapidly descending from Mt. Crumpit. Like a missile, he headed straight toward the Christmas tree along the path he'd calculated for the giant snowball. "WHOOOOAAAH!" he screamed.

But no one in *Who*-ville heard him. They were too busy counting down to the big, big moment

when the lights would go on. "TEN!" they all shouted together.

In the sky, the Grinch saw he was going to smack right into the tree. He frantically waved his arms and legs, trying to change his course.

It didn't work.

"NINE!" chanted all the *Whos*.

SCRUNCH! The Grinch flew right into the tree, up near the top. "AAUUUGH!" he shrieked as he fell down through the tree, bouncing off branches and ornaments, and getting tangled up in tinsel and strings of lights.

"EIGHT! SEVEN! SIX!" the crowd counted down.

The Grinch crashed through the Christmas dragon ornament that Bricklebaum had added to the tree, and ended up wearing it like a costume.

"FIVE!" shouted the crowd.

Dressed as the Christmas dragon and caught in more tinsel, the Grinch flew down the front of the tree.

"FOUR!" the crowd yelled louder, led by Mayor McGerkle.

"Hey, my dragon can fly!" Bricklebaum said, surprised.

"THREE!" everybody else shouted, including Cindy-Lou and Groopert from the top of the carousel.

The Grinch kept falling, getting closer and closer to the ground. "Oh-no-no-no-no!"

Mayor McGerkle reached for the giant light switch.

"TWO!" chanted all the *Whos*.

The tinsel unwrapping from around the Grinch reached its full length. As if on cue, his head knocked the light switch on, and then the tinsel yanked him back up into the tree. "Ugghh!" he groaned.

All the *Whos* stared at the huge tree. Thousands of colored lights twinkled in the crisp night air.

The Grinch dropped near the ground, his foot still caught in the shiny tinsel. "No, no, no!" he protested.

"Aw, the tree's beautiful," Bricklebaum said, his face lighting up in the warm glow of the tree.

Up on the carousel, Cindy-Lou and Groopert

stared at the tree, awestruck by its magnificence.

"Wow," Cindy-Lou said.

"Whoa," Groopert said.

Mayor McGerkle raised his hand toward the tree. "There it is!" he said. "The most beautiful tree *Who*-ville has ever seen. Everyone, have a wonderful Christmas season!"

WHUMP! Having finally kicked his foot free of the tinsel, the Grinch fell onto the stage under the tree. On his knees, he looked out at the crowd of *Whos,* all celebrating the Christmas season together. His plan had failed and this was the last place he wanted to be! He had to get out!

He slipped into the crowd, moving in the opposite direction from most of the *Whos,* like a fish swimming upstream. "No," he said to himself. "Oh, no, no."

As he struggled through the happy crowd, all the Christmas sights and sounds took him back to his childhood. That was exactly what he'd wanted to avoid. Suddenly, the Grinch remembered one terrible Christmas as though it were all happening again.

He was just a small boy, standing alone in the Who-ville orphanage, staring out through the window. He could see all the other little Whos, the ones with moms and dads, standing around that year's tree, smiling up at the lights and the ornaments.

He walked away from the window and down an empty hallway. He imagined a beautiful tree inside the orphanage, a tree decorated with shining ornaments, lit with colored lights, and surrounded by lots and lots of presents.

Then the vision faded. There was no tree. There were no presents. When it came to the young Grinch, nobody cared. He looked outside again and saw young Whos happily running toward their parents. And in that sad, lonely moment, the young Grinch realized that Christmas was the worst day of the year.

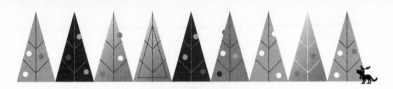

The Grinch tried to make his way through the crowd of *Whos* as quickly as possible, jostled and bumped by all the cheerful citizens. Seeing them all so happy made him feel just as wretched as he had when he was a little boy in the *Who*-ville orphanage.

Surrounded by everyone else's joy, the Grinch felt panic growing inside of him. He tried to block the awful memories from flooding his brain, but there was no stopping them.

He remembered being alone and looking through

a window into a *Who* home, and seeing the family sit down together at a big dining table to feast on *Who* Pudding and Roast Beast. And then he remembered standing alone outside in the cold winter air, listening as all the *Whos* joined hands around the town Christmas tree and started to sing together.

He knew it would happen again this year on Christmas morning. Everyone in *Who*-ville would gather around the big tree, join hands, open their mouths, and . . .

They'll sing! he thought. *And they'll sing! And they'll SING! SING! SING! SING!*

As he finally broke away from the crowd of merry *Whos*, he said to himself, "I must stop this whole thing!"

He trudged up the twisted path to his cave high on Mt. Crumpit, stomped the snow off his feet, and went in through the front door with Max. Soon the sad green Grinch was seated at the bench of his organ, his fingers idly picking out a melancholy tune. He was thinking hard. Max looked on, wondering

just what his poor master was pondering.

"Why, for fifty-three years I've put up with it now!" the Grinch complained. "I must stop this Christmas from coming! But how?"

He played another somber note on the organ. Max considered playing the drums, but looked at his master's face and thought better of it.

Then the Grinch got an idea! An awful idea! A wonderfully awful idea!

Grinning a terrible grin and snapping his furry fingers, the Grinch announced, "I know just what to do! I'm going to STEAL THEIR CHRISTMAS!"

He rushed upstairs to a window that looked out over *Who*-ville. The Grinch perched on the windowsill, delighting in his evil plan. "All the trimmings!" he said. "All the trappings! All their gifts and garlands!"

Max, who had followed him up to the window, stared at the Grinch with his eyes open wide. "When they wake and see it's gone," the Grinch told his dog, "then all their joy and happiness will be gone as well! So prepare yourself, Max! For tomorrow . . . we begin!"

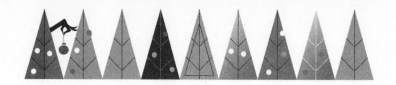

Very early the next morning, Max was sleeping on his little mattress and blue blanket when—*DING-A-LING-A-LING!* The bell rang! The Grinch was already awake!

Max quickly made his master's coffee, set it on the tray, balanced the tray on his head, and backed into the mini-elevator. He pulled the handle with his mouth, and the mini-elevator started to rise. But as it neared the Grinch's bedroom, Max heard a most unfamiliar sound—something moving on the floor above him.

DING! The mini-elevator reached the bedroom, and the nightstand door opened. When Max stepped out, he was shocked by what he saw!

The Grinch, dressed in workout clothes, was already up and exercising! As he stretched and bent, he chanted, "And squat and up, and squat and up, and squat!" He bent forward and looked at Max through his legs. "Genius starts with the abs, Max!" he explained.

After a few more squats and bends, the Grinch

stood up straight, squared his shoulders, and said, "It's go time."

The Grinch and Max got into the red chair. But instead of rising into the dining room, it took off, shooting down through a tunnel to the Grinch's basement workshop. The stony chamber was full of all kinds of equipment, gizmos, gadgets, and unfinished inventions going up, down, and in every direction. The Grinch hopped out of the chair, set Max down, and strode over to a gigantic blackboard.

"And now the question we have all been asking ourselves," he said, tapping the blackboard with his fingers. "How will I steal Christmas? Well, Max, prepare to have your little doggy mind blown!"

"ARF!" Max barked, eagerly wagging his tail.

With a grand flourish, the Grinch flipped the giant blackboard around to reveal what he'd written on the other side in the middle of the night. Max expected to see an elaborate plan, but all he saw was a familiar name written in small letters: *Santa Claus*.

"Ta-da!" the Grinch said proudly.

Max raised an eyebrow and gave a puzzled little bark. "Arf?"

"You see, I will become Santa Claus!" the Grinch explained. "But instead of *giving* all the joy and happiness, I'll take it away! If he can deliver Christmas to the whole world in one night, then I can certainly steal it from little old *Who*-ville. I mean, come on! What's Santa have that I don't?"

Max barked. "ARF!"

The Grinch frowned as he considered what Max had said, and then pointed a finger at him and replied, "That's hurtful."

11

While the Grinch was explaining his dastardly scheme to Max, Donna *Who* was in her kitchen, trying to get Buster and Bean to eat waffles. She had a fork in each hand, and each fork had a bite of waffle on it. The twins stubbornly kept their mouths tightly shut and their arms folded across their chests.

"Choo choo!" Donna said, trying to make her best train sounds. "Okay, make a tunnel! Here comes the waffle train! Open up, here it comes! Choo choo!"

RUMBLE. A bowling ball rolled through the

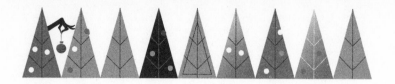

door and across the kitchen floor. Donna stared at it. Cindy-Lou ran into the kitchen after the ball.

"What are you doing with my bowling ball?" Donna asked her daughter.

"Chasing it," Cindy-Lou answered as she crossed the kitchen and then scooped up the heavy ball.

"And you're taking it where?" Donna asked.

"It's a secret," Cindy-Lou said as she headed for the door.

"All right," Donna said, relenting. "But not without breakfast! Catch!" She snatched a couple of waffles off a plate and tossed them across the kitchen to Cindy-Lou, who caught them and stuffed them into her bag.

"Whoa, waffles!" Cindy-Lou said happily. "My favorite! Thanks! See you guys later!" She strapped the bag onto her back and carried the bowling ball out the door.

The sun was up, glinting and sparkling off the clean white snow. Cindy-Lou stowed the bowling ball in her snow-bike, which she powered by pedaling when it wasn't sliding down hills on its ski. The snow-bike featured a shiny, egg-shaped sidecar so

Cindy-Lou could give a ride to a passenger.

Cindy-Lou jumped on the snow-bike and took off through the streets of Who-ville, sliding along the slick snow and ice. When she reached a certain house, she parked next to a tree, cupped her hands to her mouth, and called out, "Ka-kaw! Ka-kaw!"

A bag flew down and landed in the sidecar. Then Groopert stuck his head out a window of the house's second story. He'd heard Cindy-Lou's "Ka-kaw" (their pre-arranged secret signal) and answered with his own "Whoop whoop!" He looked from side to side, making sure the coast was clear. Then he pulled out a math textbook, opened it, and draped it over a branch of the tree just outside his window. Holding on to the front and back covers of the book, he slid down the bending branch like he was riding a zip line and dropped into the sidecar.

"Ready!" he said.

"All right," Cindy-Lou said, grinning. "Let's go!"

She stood up on the pedals, and they took off, sliding through the streets and out of Who-ville. They went into the forest on the edge of town, following a path they knew well. At one point, they

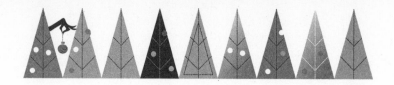

rode across a large log. When they reached the far end of the log, their weight tipped the log down.

"Hold on!" Cindy-Lou warned.

"Whoo!" they both whooped as the log fell, taking them to the next part of their secret route. Eventually they reached a huge tree with an elaborate tree fort in its branches. Cindy-Lou parked her snow-bike under the tree, and they climbed out.

"Let's go! Let's go! Let's move!" Groopert said, excited.

Two ends of a long, sturdy rope hung down from the tree fort. One end had a large, T-shaped bar tied to it with the T upside-down. The other end of the rope had a bag tied to it. Groopert dropped the bowling ball into the bag. He and Cindy-Lou climbed onto the T-bar, standing on either side and holding on to the rope. With their feet, they both kicked the bag with the bowling ball. As it fell, the weight of the bowling ball pulled the rope and the T-bar up to the tree fort!

"Hang on!" Groopert called out. "Whooooooo!" When they reached the fort, he said, "And dismount!" The two friends jumped off the T-bar

onto the wooden floor of the tree fort, high above the ground.

Cindy-Lou dug the waffles out of her backpack, put them on a plate, and poured syrup on them. As Groopert sat and ate the waffles, Cindy-Lou flipped over a sheet of paper on an easel so she had a fresh blank piece to write on. She found a marker and wrote *Santa Claus*. Then she tapped the paper with her marker.

"So," she said. "What do we know?"

"Waff-ulz er de-wicious," Groopert said, with his mouth full.

"Super delicious," Cindy-Lou agreed, "but I meant about meeting Santa Claus."

Groopert thought a moment, chewing. He swallowed and said, "We know no one's ever done it."

"Hmmm," Cindy-Lou said, thinking. "Okay, how about this? I'm gonna sit in our living room with my eyes wide open."

She opened her eyes as wide as they'd go. Staring at Groopert, she looked a little like a startled owl.

"And if I start to drift off to sleep, I'll just open my eyes wider."

"Um, I'm pretty sure you're gonna fall asleep," Groopert objected. "And by the time you wake up—"

"—he'll be gone," Cindy-Lou admitted. She knew it was true.

"Poof!" Groopert said, moving his hands like a magician revealing a missing bunny. "Nothing but cookie crumbs!"

Cindy-Lou nodded.

They sat there in silence for a moment, thinking.

Then Groopert sat up straight. "I got it!"

"Tell me!" Cindy-Lou said eagerly.

"Maple syrup!" Groopert said.

"All right," Cindy-Lou said slowly, not knowing where he was going with this. "Maple syrup . . . ?"

"We pour it on the roof," Groopert explained. "The reindeer get stuck. And then they can't fly away. Science." He folded his arms and smiled a satisfied smile.

Cindy-Lou wasn't sure about this plan. "Won't the syrup just freeze?"

"Good point," Groopert agreed, his smile fading.

Then something dawned on her. "Wait a minute!" she cried. "I THINK I'VE GOT IT!"

Excited, Cindy-Lou headed out of the tree fort.

"Where are you going?" Groopert asked.

"We're gonna need the whole gang for this one," Cindy-Lou replied.

"Okay," Groopert said. "Just let me finish my waffles."

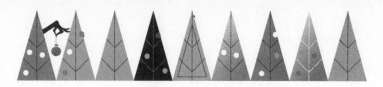

The Grinch was back in his study with Max. But this time they weren't playing chess. The Grinch ran his finger along the books on the shelves, scanning the titles, searching for a particular volume. "Aha!" he finally exclaimed, pulling a thick book down from the top shelf. *"Cringle's Christmas Almanac!"* He stopped a moment to think. "Why do I own this?" Then he remembered. "Ah, yes. Bricklebaum," the Grinch said. "He gave it to me. *Typical.*"

With the big volume tucked under his arm, the Grinch crossed over to his desk and sat down, saying,

"Okay, if I'm going to become Santa, then I need to get into character."

He started flipping through the pages. "All right, let's see. Christmas tree, Christmas traditions, Christmas pudding . . . how does pudding work its way into everything?"

From his spot on the floor, Max watched his master, not sure what exactly he was up to.

Growing a little frustrated, the Grinch said, "Where is the Santa stuff?" As he continued to turn the pages, he happened upon a picture of a happy family at Christmas. "Oh my goodness, look at this," he scoffed. "Little girls and boys giggling over sugarplums."

The Grinch felt himself being drawn into the heartwarming illustration despite himself. "Oooh, look at how they did the roof of the gingerbread house with vanilla icing," he said. "And made a little family of gumdrops!" But then he caught himself and went back into his usual sour mood. "So dumb. So, so stupidly dumb."

After turning a few more pages, the Grinch found what he was looking for.

"Ah! Here we are!" he exclaimed. *"The Legend of Santa Claus!"* He scanned the page, looking for useful information about how to portray St. Nick. "Red suit, white beard, always in a jolly mood."

"Oh . . ." He looked up from the book and spoke to Max. "Well, that's not going to happen."

The Grinch slammed the book closed, pushed his chair back, and stood up. "Oh well. Let's just start with a sleigh and go find ourselves some reindeer."

After putting on warm scarves, the Grinch and Max headed outside and down the mountain to look for reindeer. They hiked through the forest and reached an outcropping of stone that overlooked the meadows below.

The Grinch pulled out a horn decorated with elaborate carvings. "Beautiful, isn't it?" he said, showing the horn to Max. "This, my little friend, is the rein-horn. It perfectly recreates the call of the reindeer. Observe!"

He held the horn up to his lips, took a deep breath, and blew. *BAAAAAAAAH!*

The Grinch lowered the horn and waited for

reindeer to come running. But none did. After a moment, a lone goat wandered up.

"Oh," said the Grinch. "Hey there. Sorry, little goat, I was calling for a rein—"

BAAAAAAAAH! The goat screamed a tremendously loud scream!

"Aaaaah!" yelled the Grinch, startled by the goat's scream. "What was that?!" He tried to shoo the goat away with his hands. "Scram! Skedaddle, you strange goat!"

But the goat just stared at them. The Grinch and Max decided to leave this outcropping and find a new spot to call the reindeer.

Soon they'd found a promising place. Stopping to look around, the Grinch told Max, "Now, reindeer migrate, so maybe we'll catch a few headed south for the winter. I also read they tend to bed down for the night in—"

He whirled around and, without taking a breath, addressed the goat that was following them through the wilderness. "Will you stop following us?! Shoo! Away! Go back to the goat farm! Go eat a can!"

The Grinch and Max pressed on, leaving the

goat and searching for reindeer. "Ugh," the Grinch said. "Now that that's over, back to the task at hand. Ooo! It's a little crisp!"

It was more than crisp. As the Grinch and Max trudged along, the temperature plummeted, and a blizzard began to howl. "It's g-g-getting r-r-really c-c-cold!" the Grinch observed, his teeth chattering. "Can't feel my lips! Can't . . . blink. . . . Eyes frozen."

By the time they reached the peak of a mountain, the Grinch was nearly frozen solid, and Max was partially encased in a cube of ice! But when they looked down, still able to move their eyes (barely), they saw a huge herd of reindeer in the valley below!

"Max!" the Grinch managed to say. "We've hit the mother lode! We'll have a hundred reindeer to pull our—"

BAAAAAAAAAAHHHHH! The screaming goat gave one last ear-piercing scream, loud enough to blast Max and the Grinch out of their ice! At the sound of the goat's scream, all the reindeer below stampeded away.

The Grinch just stood there, shocked by what had happened. He sighed. But then, as the mist

cleared, he saw one very hairy and somewhat over-weight reindeer remaining in the valley below.

He and Max carefully made their way down into the valley, slowly approaching the big reindeer. The Grinch peered at him from behind a tree. "Well, Santa had eight," he sighed to Max. "This one looks like he ate the other seven." He went into a stealthy crouch. "Watch and learn, Max," he whispered.

Tunneling under the snow, the Grinch snuck behind the chubby reindeer as it stood still, slowly chewing on grass. The Grinch popped up out of the snow and raised a lasso in one hand. *All right,* he thought. *Now to toss this lasso around your—*

But just as the Grinch was about to throw his rope, the chunky reindeer moved, shuffling to a different spot to find more grass under the snow.

The Grinch followed the reindeer, taking up a new position behind him. "Heh heh heh," he softly chuckled to himself as he swung his lasso. He let it fly, but it just landed on the reindeer's back. The reindeer looked up from grazing, and the Grinch dove beneath the snow.

His hiding place would have been perfect except

that the tuft of green hair on the top of his head stuck out.

The reindeer ambled over to the tuft. Mistaking it for grass, the reindeer licked its lips.

CHOMP!

"AHHH!" the Grinch screamed, bursting up out of the snow and holding his new bald spot.

Terrified, the reindeer took off running, but the Grinch managed to hurl his lasso around the reindeer's neck. *TWANG!* The rope pulled tight, and the Grinch was yanked off his feet! He went flying after the reindeer, bumping over mounds of snow. "AAAAAHHHHHHGH!"

The Grinch managed to get his feet on the ground and stand up for a second, skiing over the snow. "Ha ha!" he laughed triumphantly. But seconds later—

WHAM! The Grinch slammed right into the thick trunk of a tree!

The next thing he knew, he was lying in the snow, being licked by a big, wet reindeer tongue.

13

As the sun set, the Grinch, Max, and the chubby reindeer walked across a snowy field, heading home. "Keep walking," the Grinch told his two companions. "We are headed toward destiny."

Back in *Who*-ville, Cindy-Lou had summoned the rest of her gang to meet in the town's Maze of Christmas Lights. Cindy-Lou and Groopert had gotten there first. Now they eagerly awaited the others' arrival. When she saw her friends Ozzy, Izzy, and Axl walking up, Cindy-Lou grinned. Axl, wearing a blue coat and a striped scarf, was the tallest. Ozzy

was much shorter, with goggles strapped around his warm winter hat. Shortest of all was Izzy. She wore big, round black glasses, a scarf, and earmuffs.

"All right," Ozzy said. "You called, we came."

"So, what's up?" Izzy asked.

"Yeah, what's the deal?" Axl asked.

"Thanks for getting here so fast, guys," Cindy-Lou said. "Follow me."

She took off through the maze, followed by Izzy, Ozzy, Axl, and Groopert.

"So, what's the big secret?" Axl asked as they trotted along.

"Yeah, I don't have very long," Ozzy said. "My parents set the timer."

"Dude," Axl said.

Ozzy knew what his friend meant. Something along the lines of *You're telling me your parents actually set a timer, and you have to be back home before the timer goes off or you'll be in trouble?*

"Dude" could mean a lot.

"Don't ask," Ozzy said. "It's new."

Cindy-Lou led the gang down narrow paths between high walls lit by thousands of colored lights. Kids chased each other through the maze, laughing and screaming.

The five friends passed through a tall curtain of lights into the center of the maze, where there was a giant Santa Claus made of lights.

"All right, everybody," Cindy-Lou said, "brace yourselves. In exactly forty-eight hours, we are going to do something that's never been done before." She took a deep breath. "We're gonna trap Santa Claus."

The others looked stunned. Ozzy broke the silence. "Trap Santa? Why would we want to do that?"

"Duh, to steal all the toys!" Axl said. "I love it."

Ozzy and Izzy agreed that sounded like a great idea!

"No," Cindy-Lou said quickly. "Not to steal his toys. To, um, talk to him."

"What?" Ozzy said, confused. "Why would you want to talk to him?"

"It's personal," Groopert explained.

"Yeah, it's kinda personal," Cindy-Lou confirmed.

Ozzy immediately got a stubborn look on his face. "Well, I don't want to do it if you won't tell me why," he insisted.

"What are you talking about, 'personal'?" Axl asked.

Cindy-Lou turned to him. "Axl, when you asked to borrow sixteen dollars and my mom's suitcase, did I ask you why?"

Axl thought about it. "No," he admitted.

She turned to Ozzy. "And what about you, Ozzy? Remember when you got stuck in that—"

"All right, all right, okay, geez," Ozzy said quickly to cut her off, not wanting that particular embarrassing incident brought up again.

"I did it because you're my friends," Cindy-Lou continued. "And when something matters to you, that means it matters to me."

They all stood there a moment. Then Groopert said, "That's beautiful."

"Okay, okay, okay," Axl grumbled to his friend. "You convinced me."

"Count me in, too," Ozzy said.

"All right, we're in," Izzy added.

Cindy-Lou grinned. "Great! Now let's do this! To the bikes!"

Moments later, the five friends were on their snow-bikes, breezing down the slick streets of *Who*-ville. But they hadn't gotten far when they heard their parents calling: "Let's go—dinnertime!" "Cindy-Lou, dinnertime!" "Time to eat!"

"Ooo!" Groopert said, licking his lips. "Dinner!"

They hit the brakes and came to a stop in the middle of the street. "All right," Cindy-Lou said. "We meet first thing in the morning."

"Okay," Groopert said.

"All right, see you tomorrow," Ozzy agreed.

"See you all in the morning," Axl said.

"OZZY! TIMER!" Ozzy's mother bellowed.

"Okay, Mom!" Ozzy called off, hurrying toward home. He had no interest in finding out what happened when the timer actually went off.

14

The Grinch had a reindeer. (He'd decided to call him Fred.) Now he needed a sleigh.

And he knew just where to get one.

That night, the Grinch and Max snuck through Bricklebaum's yard, hiding behind a big mound of snow. The mound of snow shifted—it was Fred in disguise!

The Grinch tried to walk through the yard as quietly as possible, but with every step, the snow made a loud *CRUNCH*. "This is the loudest snow I've ever heard in my life," he muttered.

When they got close to the house, all lit up with Christmas lights, the Grinch pointed up to the roof. "See up there?" he asked Max and Fred. "That's our sleigh."

Max and Fred both looked at the huge sleigh on top of Bricklebaum's roof. Then they shared a doubtful look. How were they going to get it down without anyone noticing?

"You two go around back," the Grinch instructed them. "Wait for me to drop the sleigh from the roof. Okay—go, team!"

As Max and Fred headed around to the back of Bricklebaum's house, the Grinch tiptoed through the snow toward a ladder that Bricklebaum had left outside. But as the Grinch passed the house, he saw Bricklebaum's dog, Mabel, sleeping on the other side of a doggy door. She was round and gray, and she wore a pink bow. "Oh!" the Grinch said quietly. "Shhh!"

He carefully picked up the ladder and set it against the house, keeping an eye on the sleeping dog. But when he tried to climb the ladder, it sank into the snow under his weight. "No!" he cried. "No, no, no!"

That woke Mabel. She looked out and saw the Grinch. The would-be thief laughed nervously.

Mabel came tearing out through the doggy door and started nipping at the Grinch's heels. "Ow!" he yelped. "Ahh!"

The Grinch pulled himself up onto a balcony. Mabel ran back into the house. "Whew!" the Grinch said, stopping to catch his breath. But then Mabel stuck her head out of a window by the balcony, looking for the intruder. "Ahh!" the Grinch yelled.

Mabel hopped out the window, chasing the Grinch. He ran from her and slipped. He kicked his dangling feet, accidentally pressing a doorbell. *DING-DONG!*

Grimacing, the Grinch finally managed to scramble up to the edge of a gutter. Down below, Mabel barked up at him. "RARF! RARF!"

WHOMP! A big pile of snow fell off the roof and onto Mabel, momentarily burying her. As the Grinch clung to the gutter, Bricklebaum came out to see who had rung his doorbell. "Who's there?" he asked into the darkness. "What's going on?"

The Grinch's fingers were giving out one by one,

and he was about to fall, when Mabel popped up out of the snow in front of Bricklebaum. "Hey, who taught Mabel how to use the doorbell?" Bricklebaum asked. "Man, that's awesome! You smart little dog!" He scooped Mabel up, kissed the top of her head, and carried her back into the warm house.

Straining and grunting, the Grinch managed to pull himself up and continue his climb toward the roof. As he passed a window, he paused to look inside. "Eh, what's this?"

Bricklebaum and his party guests were earnestly singing a classic Christmas song. The Grinch stared at them through the window. Part of him longed to be inside with them. But he shook his head and continued climbing.

Through another window, Mabel spotted the Grinch. Growling, she raced out of the room to find the intruder. Bricklebaum didn't notice her exit. He was too busy picking the next song to be sung.

Moments later, the Grinch pulled himself onto the roof. He crossed to the sleigh and looked down at Max and Fred waiting in the backyard. "All right!" he hissed down to them. "Here it comes! Get

ready! Easy as taking candy from a baby."

Holding on to the chimney, he bent down to unhook the cords tying the sleigh to the roof and saw Mabel, teeth bared, snarling. "Grrrrr—"

"Uh," the Grinch said, "good puppy?"

Mabel launched herself at the Grinch! He let go of the chimney and slid down the roof. With the sleigh's cords unhooked, it fell, hitting a balcony on its way down.

The Grinch swung into Bricklebaum's house through a window, with Mabel in his arms. No one saw him, and he tossed Mabel aside. The little dog sailed past party guests, snagging their cocoa and cake. She came to a stop on a table, right in front of Bricklebaum. "Look at that!" Bricklebaum exclaimed, laughing. "Mabel is delivering cakes now! I mean, is this the best Christmas ever, or what?"

Outside, the sleigh had fallen to the ground. The Grinch plunged out a window, ending up in the seat next to Max. Fred took off, pulling the large sleigh.

Through his window, Bricklebaum caught a glimpse of the sleigh gliding away in the distance. "Wow!" he said. "I think I just saw Santa Claus!"

15

Back in his cave, the Grinch got ready for bed with a spring in his step. "Today was great!" he announced. "We did mean things and we did them in style!"

As he climbed into bed, he looked down at the floor and saw Max staring up at him with big eyes. "Max, don't do puppy eyes," he scolded. "You know the rules. You sleep in your bed, and I sleep in—"

As he turned away, he found himself face to face with Fred! "WAAH!" the Grinch shouted, startled to find the reindeer staring at him from the other side of the bed. "Fred! Okay, please

tell me you're kidding. No! No, no!"

Fred tried to climb onto the bed. The Grinch tried to push him away, but Fred was big and heavy. And he wanted to be in the bed. After some wrestling, the Grinch succeeded in shoving Fred off the bed.

Fred stared at him with sad eyes.

And so did Max.

"Oh no," the Grinch said. "Not you, too. I don't believe this. Max, did you teach Fred puppy eyes?"

They both kept staring at him with their big, sad eyes.

"Fine," the Grinch sighed. "This one time."

Max and Fred hopped into the Grinch's bed. Though it was crowded, they all got comfortable and settled down to sleep. Soon, the Grinch was snoring. No one, much less the Grinch himself, would have guessed it, but there was a smile on his face.

The next morning, Fred walked into the kitchen. He spotted the complicated coffee machine.

Moments later, Max headed in to make coffee for the Grinch. He froze when he saw Fred balanced

on the machine, trying to make a cup himself! The chubby reindeer stepped on the plunger, and the coffee poured into the cup.

Fred smiled. And Max sighed in relief.

A little later, the Grinch, Fred, and Max sat at the dining room table eating breakfast. "Mmm," the Grinch said appreciatively. "Now, THAT is a great cup of coffee!"

Fred smiled again. Max narrowed his eyes, as if to say, "Making coffee is MY job!"

"Max," the Grinch said to his faithful pup, "this morning you and I need to gather some information. Fred, you just sit right there . . . and don't touch anything!"

A little later, the Grinch and Max stood on the cliff just outside the cave's front door. Looking uncertain, Max wore a harness with several propellers. On his head was a cluster of cameras.

The Grinch stood next to a monitor, wearing a headset microphone. "Okay, Max," he said. "I'll be in your ear the whole time, and whatever you're seeing, I'll be seeing on the monitor. Ready?"

Despite the Grinch's calm explanation, Max still

looked unsure about the whole thing. The Grinch pressed a button on his remote control. The propellers started to spin. "Now off you go, Max!" the Grinch said. "Fly, boy! Fly!"

Toggling the switches on the controller, the Grinch sent Max soaring off toward *Who*-ville. In his earpiece, Max could still hear the Grinch's voice. "If we are going to steal Christmas, we need to know as much about *Who*-ville as possible. How many houses are in *Who*-ville? How many *Whos*? How many wreaths and trees? How many chimneys?"

Flying between two birds, Max smiled at one of the birds. The bird looked confused.

Thanks to the camera, the Grinch could see exactly what Max was looking at. "No," he chided. "Stop socializing. Now, let's go in for a look."

Max swooped in over the houses of *Who*-ville. "Okay," the Grinch said. "Twelve houses on Elm Street. That means— Oh! Watch out!"

Max came too close to a *Who* in the bucket of a crane. He was putting up Christmas decorations. "Huh?" said the *Who*. "What was that?"

Max quickly flew around a corner, out of the

Who's sight. The man shrugged and went back to his work, humming a holiday tune.

"Okay," the Grinch said to Max through the headset. "Go, go, go."

Emerging from his hiding place, Max flew down the street. "Now cut through Main Street," the Grinch ordered, "and survey the south side."

Max swooped down Main Street, flying above all the *Who* shoppers without anyone looking up and noticing him. "Look at those greedy little gift monsters loading themselves up with Christmas junk," the Grinch sneered. "It's all they care about."

When Max reached the end of the block, the Grinch said, "Okay, Max, turn right here!" As Max buzzed over the street, Bricklebaum passed below him. He was telling a friend, "So I woke up this morning, got dressed, had my coffee, went outside, looked on the roof, and my sleigh was gone! A mystery!"

Listening on his headset, the Grinch grinned. "My, my. I wonder who took it!"

Suddenly, Max spotted something interesting in front of one of the shops. He flew toward it.

At that moment, the Grinch was calculating: "If

we do twenty-eight houses an hour for six hours, that would be . . . sausages?"

His monitor was filled with strings of sausages getting closer and closer. Max clearly was flying straight for them. "No," the Grinch barked. "Don't even think about it!"

But Max couldn't resist delicious sausages. As he flew by, he craned his neck around and bit the nearest sausage. The whole string of sausages came loose, getting caught in Max's propellers! His flying gizmo wobbled out of control!

"MAAAAAXXX!" the Grinch yelled.

Max swooped and dipped and whipped around *Who*-ville! "Whoa!" the Grinch said. "Max, are you okay?"

He stared at the monitor, trying to figure out where Max was. "Max?"

He saw something green and furry on the monitor—small at first, but getting bigger and bigger. It looked like his back! "Oh hey, look! It's me!" the Grinch cried. "AHHHH!"

He turned around and Max walloped right into him—*WHAM!*—sending the Grinch flying.

16

The Grinch and Max went back inside the cave. "Mission accomplished!" the Grinch sang out. "Fred!"

Looking for the reindeer, the Grinch and Max headed into the kitchen. It was a complete mess! "Fred! What are you doing?" the Grinch cried.

Fred looked at them. He was sucking on the nozzle of a can of whipped cream. Whipped cream shot out of his nose, and he sniffed it back in.

The Grinch sighed. "Come on, Max. We've got work to do."

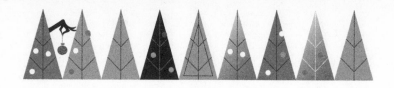

The Grinch had converted one of the cave's bigger chambers into a command center for his Stealing Christmas operation, complete with a detailed model of *Who*-ville. He stuck a spool of red yarn on Fred's antler. "Now let's plan our route," the Grinch said.

He grabbed the end of the red yarn and pulled, tacking down a route through the model town. The spool spun quickly, letting out more yarn as the Grinch raced around the model. "First we go south. Quick jaunt to the east. And then this house—skip the subdivision for the moment—knock off the entire southeast quadrant, and"—the Grinch stuck his last tack in the model version of Cindy-Lou *Who*'s house—"then we finish it all up on Whistling-*Who* Lane. That's 223 houses and only seven hours of darkness to work with. That means we have to be FAST and FOCUSED!"

The Grinch paced back and forth in front of Max and Fred like a general addressing his troops. "There will be temptation all around us!" he barked.

He dramatically pressed a button. Slowly a

curtain opened, revealing a gorgeous, elaborate mock-up of a living room decorated for Christmas, including a tree with lots of presents under it.

"Behold," the Grinch said, "the present!" He grabbed a wrapped gift with a bow around it from under the tree. He looked at the shining box with great distrust. "This is our enemy. You will want to unwrap it and play with it. You'll think it would be fun. Lots of fun . . ." For a moment, it looked as though the Grinch was thinking about doing those very things. But he quickly regained his steely composure. "But you must not! And after you get past the present, a challenging obstacle still remains. . . ."

He held up a red sprinkle cookie shaped like a Christmas tree. It looked absolutely scrumptious. "The cookie! Look at it in all its red sugary splendor. . . ."

Staring, Max and Fred moved toward the cookie with their tongues hanging out.

"No, no, no!" the Grinch warned, shaking his head.

Max and Fred were still staring and drooling.

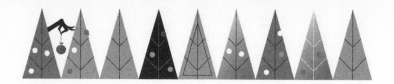

"Discipline!" the Grinch snapped. "We must—"

CHOMP!

Fred took the whole cookie in one big bite.

"—resist," the Grinch concluded, sighing.

In Cindy-Lou's house, the gang had gathered in the living room. Cindy-Lou knelt in front of the fireplace. "Are you ready?" she called up into the inky darkness.

"Almost," came Groopert's voice echoing down the tall chimney.

"Good," Cindy-Lou said. "Think jolly."

"And fat!" Ozzy added.

There was a moment of silence.

"Okay," Groopert called down. "I'm ready."

Cindy-Lou turned to Ozzy, Izzy, and Axl. "All right, quick! Everybody hide!"

The four friends ran behind the sofa. "Three, two, one, cue Santa!" Cindy-Lou yelled.

Nothing happened.

"That means you, Groopert," Cindy-Lou explained.

"WAAAAH!" Groopert yelled as he tumbled down through the chimney. *CLUNK!* He hit the bottom and rolled out of the fireplace into the living room. He was dressed as Santa and appeared a little blackened and battered.

Groopert stood up and looked around. Speaking in his best Santa voice, he said, "Ho, ho, ho, ho! Look at this pretty house! I will leave presents for the people!"

"Come on," Ozzy said, reacting to Groopert's line delivery. "It's not the school play, dude."

"Then why do I have to wear the outfit?" Groopert asked, not unreasonably.

"Groopert, focus!" Cindy-Lou said. "Just get the cookie."

Groopert glanced across the room. He saw a chocolate-chip cookie sitting inside a carefully drawn white chalk circle next to a sign that read FOR SANTA. He walked over to it. He reached toward the cookie, then hesitated. "But I can see the string," he objected.

"Stop worrying," Izzy said. "It'll be dark at night."

"What if he has a flashlight?" Groopert asked.

Cindy-Lou made a face. "Have you ever seen a picture of Santa with a flashlight?"

"No," Groopert admitted, "but I just think he might—"

"Groopert," Cindy-Lou said firmly. "Just pick up the cookie!"

Groopert went back to his Santa voice. "Ho, ho, ho, what do we have here? A delicious little cookie!" He grabbed it and—*SWOOP!*—A rope yanked him out of the room! "AHHHH!" he screamed.

The other kids saw Groopert crash out the window! They ran to it and looked out. "Groopert!" Cindy-Lou called.

But instead of Groopert, only his clothes were hanging from the branch of a tree. "Groopert?" Cindy-Lou repeated, confused.

"Uh, hey, guys?" a voice said from behind them. They whipped around and saw Groopert standing in front of the fireplace in his underwear. He was holding the cookie. "Do I still get to eat the cookie?"

The **Grinch** lives
high on Mt. Crumpit
with his best—and
only—friend, **Max**.
The Grinch
hates Christmas.

The **Grinch** does **not** like waking up
to the sounds of Christmas music and joy.

Max informs his friend that there is
no more food in the house . . .

. . . so, like it
or not, they
will have
to go into
Who-ville.

The Grinch's neighbor covers his house in decorations,
including a giant Santa sleigh.
The Grinch thinks this might **come in handy** later.

Who-ville is so festive and full of Christmas cheer, it's **revolting**.

A girl named **Cindy-Lou** has a letter for Santa Claus. She is asking for something really **special** this year.

But little does Cindy-Lou or the rest of *Who*-ville know that while they sleep . . .

. . . the Grinch
has come up
with a
terrible plan . . .

. . . for the whole town.

He is going to
steal Christmas!

17

Up on Mt. Crumpit, the Grinch stood with Max and Fred next to something big covered by a tarp. "All right," he said proudly. "So, I tinkered with our sleigh a bit. Behold!"

He whipped off the tarp, revealing Brickle-baum's sleigh, to which the Grinch had added a miniature sidecar. "Look at this, Max! You'll be riding in style. A throne for a barking prince! How do you like that?"

Wagging his tail happily, Max jumped into the sidecar.

The Grinch led Fred to the sleigh's harness. "All right, Fred. You are the engine of this great machine. Understood?"

Fred's face stayed exactly the same.

"Good," said the Grinch.

Fred stepped into the harness. The Grinch gave his two assistants a quick pep talk. "Now, remember: this is just a practice run. But on this team we practice like we play! So let's leave it all out on the snow!"

Max barked his agreement. The Grinch climbed into the sleigh and took up the reins. He pressed a button, and a segmented mechanical arm shot out and grabbed Fred's tail. *ZHWOOM!* They took off across the snow! "Oooooh!" the Grinch whooped. "All right!"

Moving at a casual clip, Fred pulled the sleigh along a mountain path—up, down, and around a bend. "Now let's pick up the pace and see how it handles!" the Grinch said, shaking the reins. "ARF! ARF!" Max barked as Fred broke into a gallop.

"Whooooooah!" the Grinch shouted.

Enjoying himself, Fred ran even faster, taking curves like a champ. But as the sleigh rounded the

edge of another cliff, it tipped dangerously. "Whoa, hold on!" the Grinch shouted.

Fred skittered across a frozen pond and wove between trees, going faster and faster!

"Ha ha!" the Grinch laughed. "We're doing it, Max! We are doing it! We will not be—"

SCREECH! Fred came to a sudden halt. The Grinch slammed into the front of the sleigh. WHAM!

"What happened?" the Grinch asked. "Fred?"

Then he saw two reindeer walking toward them, an adult female and a baby. The Grinch got out of the sleigh and told them, "Sorry, we don't need any more reindeer."

But the two reindeer kept coming.

"No!" the Grinch shouted, flicking his hands at them. "Go! Get! Shoo! I have what I need!"

Behind him, the Grinch heard a loud reindeer call, full of joy. He turned and saw Fred with his chin lifted and his mouth wide open, bugling. An answering call came from the female deer. The Grinch looked confused. But then the two reindeer walked right up to Fred, and all three lovingly nuzzled each other. For a moment, the Grinch felt

warm and fuzzy inside seeing them together. Finally, he understood.

This was Fred's family.

"It's okay, Fred," the Grinch sighed. He undid the harness, and Fred walked away with his family. The Grinch watched them go.

"On our own again, Max," he said. Max smiled and wagged his tail. The Grinch couldn't help but smile back.

The next morning, on the day before Christmas, *Whos* were happily finishing up their last-minute shopping in downtown *Who*-ville. Carolers sang Christmas carols, and *Who* families, including Cindy-Lou's, had their Christmas portraits taken.

"All right," Donna said as they posed for the photographer. "Everyone ready?"

They all smiled. *FLASH!* And another picture-perfect moment was captured.

The forecast was for more snow—wonderful

Christmas weather. It looked as though this was going to be the best Christmas of all!

Except . . .

Up on Mr. Crumpit, the Grinch was putting the finishing touches on his nasty plan. *DING-A-LING!* The bell woke Max bright and early. He cocked his head, listening carefully. The ringing wasn't coming from the Grinch's bedroom. It was coming from the workshop!

Max made a cup of coffee, balanced the tray on his head, and hurried through the stony halls to the workshop. When he pushed the door open, he saw the Grinch, looking a bit frazzled and wild-eyed, as though he'd been up all night—which he had.

"Max!" the Grinch cried. "There you are! Check this out!"

He held up his furry feet. He was wearing extendo-shoes, which lowered as he walked toward Max. Max was amazed! It was as though the Grinch had automatic ladders built into his shoes to lift and lower him. "I have been up all night making stuff to

help us with our magnificent plan! Oooo ... more coffee!"

He eagerly lifted the cup off the tray on Max's head and sipped the hot coffee. "It's gonna be a big night," he said. "Very exciting! And speaking of exciting, I've got some great news for you. Come with me!"

He scooped Max up in his arms and carried him outside. Then the Grinch plopped his dog down in front of the sleigh. "Max, do you know what you are? You are a sturdy little fella. And loyal. Very loyal. In fact, I think you're the best dog a Grinch could hope for."

From behind his back, he pulled out a single antler and presented it to Max as the ultimate award. "And that is why I'm promoting you! Max, you will guide my sleigh tonight!"

The Grinch balanced the antler on top of Max's head and tied it on with red string. "Can you feel the excitement?" he asked.

"ARF! ARF!" Max barked excitedly.

"Ha ha!" the Grinch laughed. "I knew you wouldn't let me down!"

The Grinch spent the rest of the day getting ready. He put together his Santa suit and tried it on, checking himself out in the mirror.

He liked what he saw!

And then, not a moment too soon for all the *Who* children (and their parents, too, for that matter), it was Christmas Eve.

Shopkeepers rushed to close their stores and hurry home. Everyone was eager to get inside their houses on the most magical night of the year.

And, for once, kids were eager to go to bed.

In his room, Groopert looked out the window, sitting next to his teddy bear, Mr. Ruggles. "Now we have to stay awake," Groopert told his beloved bear. "Christmas history is about to be made."

Ozzy was in his own bedroom, running around in circles. Downstairs, his mother could hear his foot-steps. *THUMP! THUMP! THUMP! THUMP!* "Ozzy, what are you DOING?" she yelled up to him.

"Trying to get myself tired!" the boy called down to her breathlessly. "Whew!"

Izzy also wanted Christmas morning to come as soon as possible. She was already lying in bed. She was saying to herself, "All right. Eight hours until Christmas morning. That's 28,800 seconds. Okay. Aaaaaaand . . . sleep!"

Axl knelt by his bed, praying. "Please let me get what I want," he said quietly. "Please let me get what I want. Please let me get what I want."

Despite his efforts to stay awake, Groopert soon fell asleep with his face pressed against his bedroom window. Mr. Ruggles's face was pressed against the glass, too, next to him.

One by one, the bedroom lights in *Who*-ville went off, until there was only one small window light left shining in the whole town.

19

The light was in Cindy-Lou *Who*'s bedroom. She sat up on her bed, staring out the window at the starry sky. She was so excited. She could hardly wait for Santa to come flying over *Who*-ville in his magic sleigh. She'd be ready for him!

Her walkie-talkie buzzed, and Groopert's voice came through. "Waffle One, this is Waffle Two. Are you there? Over."

Cindy-Lou picked up her walkie-talkie and pressed the button. "I read you loud and clear, Waffle Two."

"This is Groopert, by the way."

"Yeah, I got that."

"Good luck tonight. I can't believe you're gonna meet Santa Claus."

"Thanks!" Cindy-Lou said. "Talk tomorrow."

Donna came into Cindy-Lou's room. "So," she asked, smiling at her daughter staring out the window. "You got any last-minute wishes for Santa?"

"Yup," Cindy-Lou said, nodding her head. "I have one great big wish."

"Good," her mom said. "Because you deserve everything you want and more."

Cindy-Lou smiled at her. "Thanks, Mom. I want the same thing for you."

Donna crossed the room and sat on the edge of Cindy-Lou's bed. "How did I end up with such a wonderful daughter?"

"I don't know," Cindy-Lou said, shrugging. "Sometimes you just get lucky."

"Well, then I really did."

"Me too."

They hugged. "I love you, Mom."

"I love you, sweetie," Donna said. "Good night."

"Good night!" Cindy-Lou replied. Donna stood up and headed for the door. She switched off the light and left.

After waiting a couple of moments, Cindy-Lou slipped out of bed and snuck out of her room. She had a trap to set.

Up on Mt. Crumpit, the Grinch climbed aboard his sleigh, full of purpose and confidence. He looked down at the quiet village of *Who*-ville, the target of his malicious plan. He took a deep breath, picked up the reins, and said, "Here we go, Max!"

He gave the reins a hearty shake. Wearing his single antler, Max leaned into his harness, working his little legs back and forth with tremendous energy. He slowly disappeared down into the snow.

The Grinch leaned forward, looking at the spot where Max had just been standing. "Max!" he cried. "Max, are you okay?"

After a moment, Max reappeared, digging his way up out of the snow. Giving it everything he had, he tried again. He pulled against the weight of

the heavy sled, slowly dragging it behind him down the mountain. As they inched forward, the Grinch laughed in triumph.

"Ha! Yes, Max! Attaboy! Go, boy, go!"

Picking up speed, the sleigh slid down the mountainside toward *Who*-ville and its twinkling Christmas lights. Soon, the Grinch and Max reached the town. They skimmed down a quiet street and came to a stop next to their first house. Following the route he'd marked on his model, the Grinch would begin stealing Christmas *right here.*

He hopped off the sleigh, and he and Max snuck closer to the house. "You take the outside," the Grinch whispered, "and I'll take the inside."

He pressed a button on Max's antler and— *CLICK*—a grappling hook popped out. Then he reached inside one of his bags and pressed another button. *SHUUUUUWOOP!* A ladder extended from the bag. The Grinch jumped on and rode the ladder up to the roof.

"Okay, house number one," he said as he snuck across the snowy roof to the chimney. Using a set of helicopter-like rotary blades with a candy-cane

handle, he floated down the chimney, through the fireplace, and out into the house. He barely even got any soot on his red Santa suit.

He landed in the middle of the living room floor, turned off his candy cane, and looked around. He took it all in—the tree, the presents, the decorations.

Satisfied, the Grinch smiled. Then he said to himself, "Okay. Now let's steal Christmas."

20

The Grinch began by holding one of his special bags open and sweeping presents into it with his big candy cane. Once he'd bagged up all the gifts, he took out a shrinking gadget he'd invented for just this purpose and aimed it at the bags— *ZZHWORK!*—instantly shrinking all the bulging bags down to a manageable size. Then he used his extending ladder to whisk the little bags up the chimney to the roof. One by one, they flew out of the chimney and landed in the snow. *PLOP! PLOP! PLOP!*

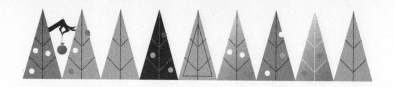

Meanwhile, outside the house, Max was using the grappling hook attached to his head to quickly strip all the Christmas lights from along the roof and around the windows. Within seconds he'd removed every single bulb and cord. The house was now dark.

Back inside, the Grinch tossed martial arts throwing stars—*ZWICK! ZWICK! ZWICK!*—at the Christmas tree, tying it into a bundle with attached wires. Using his extending ladder again, he sent the tree up the chimney and onto the roof.

The Grinch looked around the room. He'd successfully picked the whole house clean in a matter of seconds. There wasn't a single sign of Christmas cheer to be seen anywhere! He grinned an evil grin and rode his ladder up the chimney to the roof, pulling the ladder up behind him. *ZWIP!*

This was when the extendo-shoes he'd invented came in handy. By extending the soles of his shoes, he was able to simply walk from one roof to the next! In no time at all, he was down the next house's chimney and into the living room. For a moment, he stood with two candy canes crossed in front of his chest. Then, with a quick move he'd practiced back

in his cave, he used the candy canes to throw nets around all the presents piled under the tree. He reeled them in like a big school of fish.

To move even faster, the Grinch rode a tricycle before he bagged it up, zipping past a delicious-looking cookie set out on a table for Santa. He stuck to his training—he would not be distracted!

Soon he'd cleaned out the second house. He and Max moved on to the next, and the next, and the next. . . .

Using his clever inventions, the Grinch, together with Max, moved faster and faster, zooming from house to house, leaving each one picked clean. And as they got better and better at using their tools, it took them less and less time to strip all the holiday cheer out of a *Who* home.

Each time they finished a house, a counter on the sleigh ticked down by one. 154, 153, 152, 151 . . . Until finally, after several hours of nighttime thievery, the counter on the sleigh clicked down to 001. In all of *Who*-ville, there was only one house left with Christmas presents, stockings, and decorations.

Cindy-Lou *Who*'s house.

The Grinch and Max pulled up to the house in the sleigh. It was easy to spot, because it was the last house in *Who*-ville that still had any Christmas lights on it, including a beautiful tree covered in lights and ornaments.

"This is it!" the Grinch said, grinning. "The last house."

Savoring the moment, he climbed out of the sleigh, absentmindedly giving Max a pat. Then he reached down and pressed a button on his extendo-shoes. *CLICK-CLICK-CLICKETY-CLICK-CLACK!* The built-in ladders extended, shooting him up to the roof. At this point, he'd made this move so many times, he didn't feel in the least bit nervous about the height or the speed or the winter wind blowing in his face as he rose up to the top of the house.

He crossed the roof to the chimney, leaving a trail of extendo-shoe prints in the snow. Pulling out his candy-cane propeller, he climbed onto the chimney, turned on the spinning candy cane, and floated down the chimney.

The Grinch popped out of the fireplace and looked around. He started with the tree, wrapping

it up with wires and preparing to send the bundle up the chimney. Then, across the room, he noticed something . . . an extremely delicious-looking, beautifully decorated Christmas cookie sitting on a plate. It had obviously been left out for Santa.

"Ah, what a gorgeous cookie," he said to himself. Then he remembered his lecture to Max and Fred. Even in the face of great temptation, one must remain disciplined! One must resist!

But that was just to make sure they hit all the houses in one night. And they'd done it! Surely, having done such an incredible job of thievery, he deserved just one little cookie!

"Oh, what the heck," the Grinch said as he crossed the room to the plate.

He quickly snatched the beautiful cookie, and—*Wha–!?*—Cindy-Lou's trap was sprung! A WELCOME, SANTA! sign swung into place, dangling on strings.

In Cindy-Lou's bedroom, a bell over her bed rang. *DING-A-LING-A-LING!* She instantly woke up (just as Groopert had suspected, she hadn't been able to stay awake).

"It worked!" she cried. "My trap worked!"

21

As the Grinch stared at the WELCOME, SANTA! sign, bright lights blazed on all around the sign! *FWOOOM!* Blinded by the dazzling lights, the Grinch stumbled back. A rope dropped down from a fan, wrapped around his furry green ankle, and yanked the Grinch up toward the ceiling! "AAAAAHHH!" he yelled.

Dangling in the air, the Grinch struggled to free himself. Upstairs, a light snapped on. The Grinch looked at it, panicking. He mustn't be caught stealing Christmas!

Cindy-Lou peeked around the corner. "Santa Claus," she said quietly, amazed to have actually caught the famous gift-giver.

The Grinch kept shifting and wiggling, hoping to break free of Cindy-Lou's trap. Maybe he could still run away without having to talk to anyone! But then he spotted Cindy-Lou tiptoeing cautiously down the stairs.

"Oh, hello," the Grinch said, trying to sound casual and calm, the way he imagined a little girl might think Santa would sound. "Could you give me a little help, please?"

"I'll let you down," Cindy-Lou assured him. "Just give me a minute!"

"Ah, that would be great," the Grinch said.

Cindy-Lou hurried down the staircase, saying, "I'm coming! Just trying to remember which is the release cord!" When she reached the bottom of the stairs, she undid her trap. *THUMP!* The Grinch fell from the ceiling fan and hit the floor. "There we go!" Cindy-Lou said, running to help untangle him from the rope. She handed him the glass of milk by the cookie plate. "Drink this. It'll make you feel better."

Dazed, the Grinch reached for the glass and drank the cold milk. For a moment, he was lost in how delicious it was—but he snapped back to his senses when Cindy-Lou spoke again.

"Santa, I know you're busy," she said, repeating the words she'd rehearsed dozens of times, preparing for just this moment. "But there's something really important that I need—"

Suddenly Cindy-Lou stopped her prepared speech. She'd noticed something: their beautiful Christmas tree, bound by netting and stuffed partway up the chimney! "Wait," she said, confused. "Why are you taking our Christmas tree?"

The Grinch stood up, busted. Could he just run away? No, that wouldn't do. He had to think, and he had to think quickly. He needed to come up with a believable reason Santa would stuff a perfectly good Christmas tree up a chimney. "Well," he lied, "one of the lights on your tree wasn't working, so I thought I'd take it back to my workshop and see if I could fix it."

"I didn't know you did that," Cindy-Lou said. She'd heard a lot of stories about Santa Claus, but

none of them had included light-bulb repair.

"All the time. Just a little service I like to provide. Call me a perfectionist. Now why don't you go back upstairs to bed, and then when you wake up, the tree will be fixed and your presents will be waiting under it."

He tried to turn Cindy-Lou around and scoot her back toward the stairway.

"Wait, you don't understand," she said, resisting. "I don't want presents."

"Of course you do," the Grinch insisted, gently pushing her along. "Everyone wants presents."

"No, no, really I don't," Cindy-Lou said, slipping away and turning around to face him. "I want you to help my mom!"

The Grinch looked surprised. "Your mom?"

"Yeah," Cindy-Lou said, getting back to what she had planned to say to Santa. "She works so hard and is always doing stuff for other people . . . and my brothers . . . and me. And I just want her to be happy."

Stunned, the Grinch stared at the little *Who*. The thoughtfulness of Cindy-Lou's request touched

him, but he was so unfamiliar with the feeling that he didn't even realize what was happening. "You want me to help your mom?" he asked.

Cindy-Lou nodded, smiling up at him. "You're Santa. You make people happy. And everyone should be happy, right?"

The Grinch was so surprised by this whole conversation that he really had no idea what to say. He just stood there, looking into Cindy-Lou's big eyes. "Yeah," he finally muttered. "I guess they should."

To Cindy-Lou, Santa sounded sad. "Santa, are you okay?" she asked.

The Grinch tried to snap out of his gloomy thoughts about never really getting to be happy, even way back when he was just a little Grinch. Especially way back when he was just a little Grinch!

"What? Me?" he said, clearing his throat and trying to sound cheerful. "I'm fine! Now why don't you go back to bed, okay?"

"Okay," Cindy-Lou agreed. She'd said what she'd planned to say, so she couldn't do anything more.

Now it was up to Santa to see what he could do to make her mom happy.

The Grinch ushered her toward the steps. She hurried up a few and then turned around. She was still worried about how sad Santa had seemed. "I wish you could celebrate with us tomorrow," she said. "We all get together and sing. And it's so beautiful that if you close your eyes and listen, all your sadness just goes away." She closed her eyes, remembering other Christmases.

The Grinch looked at the little *Who* standing on the stairway with her eyes closed. "That sounds nice," he said. And he meant it. It did sound nice.

"Good night," Cindy-Lou said. She leaned forward and hugged the Grinch. "Thank you, Santa. For everything."

The Grinch just stood there. When was the last time anyone had hugged him? Had anyone ever hugged him?

"Good night," he said quietly.

22

When Cindy-Lou was back upstairs in her bed, the Grinch, lost in thought, mechanically turned back to the tree and stuffed it up the chimney. Then he used his candy cane to rise up the chimney.

Up on the roof, he slid the last sack and the tree down to Max, who was waiting in the yard below. The Grinch used his extendo-shoes to step off the roof and lower himself to the ground. He climbed into the sleigh and looked around at the darkened houses of *Who*-ville.

He'd done it. He'd stolen Christmas. So why didn't

he feel triumphant? Gleeful? Deliciously mean?

"I just met the strangest little *Who* girl," the Grinch told Max.

His loyal dog looked back at him, concerned. What was the matter with his master?

The Grinch shook himself and clicked the counter down to zero. "All right, Max," he said, picking up the reins. "Let's go."

Straining, Max leaned into his harness, taking one step at a time, inching forward. It helped that the streets of *Who*-ville were slippery with ice and snow. Soon the loaded sleigh was making its way through the dark town missing all its Christmas decorations.

As he rode out of town toward the base of Mt. Crumpit, the Grinch couldn't stop thinking about what the little *Who* girl had said. Could it really be that simple? Could closing your eyes and listening to a song really make all your sadness go away?

Early the next morning, as the sun rose over the snowy village of *Who*-ville, Cindy-Lou sat up in bed

and rubbed the sleep from her eyes. Then her brain kicked in and she remembered: it was Christmas morning! *CHRISTMAS!*

She jumped out of bed and ran downstairs to the living room.

Empty! No presents, no decorations, no tree.

"What?!" she asked, stunned. She stood there, staring, unable to believe what she was seeing. It had to be a cruel joke or a stupid prank.

Smiling, Donna walked into the living room. But when she saw everything gone, her smile quickly disappeared. "Oh no," she said. "What happened?"

That's exactly what every *Who* in town wanted to know. They wandered out of their houses in shock. As they looked around, they saw that all the Christmas decorations and lights were gone from the outsides of their houses, too. All of it—gone!

Instinctively, everyone headed toward the town square. Passing all the undecorated houses and shops, they were all asking themselves the same question: Who could have done such an awful, nasty, no-good, rotten thing?

As she stood in the center of the square with the other sad and bewildered *Whos*, Cindy-Lou realized she just might know the answer to that question.

Up on Mt. Crumpit, the Grinch and Max were dragging the overloaded sleigh to the very top of the very highest, tip-top peak. When they got there, they were going to shove the sleigh over the edge. It would plummet through the crisp morning air and land on the jagged rocks far below, where no one could possibly retrieve it. Every present, every tree, and every decoration would be smashed and broken. Christmas, at least for one year, would disappear in one big crash.

"Keep going, Max," the Grinch said, full of grim determination. "We're gonna make it."

The *Whos* kept pouring into the town square. Cindy-Lou spotted her friends looking dumbfounded. "Oh dear," Ozzy said when he saw that the

decorations were even gone from the square.

"What happened?" Izzy asked.

"Where are the decorations?" Ozzy asked.

"All the presents?" Groopert muttered.

"Aw, man," Axl said sadly.

Cindy-Lou just bowed her head, not knowing what to say. She turned to Donna. "Mom," she said, "it's my fault."

Donna looked puzzled. "What is?"

"All of this," Cindy-Lou said, gesturing toward the undecorated square and all the shocked citizens. "I trapped Santa last night so I could talk to him, and it must have made him mad so he stole everyone's Christmas."

Donna put her hands on her daughter's small shoulders and knelt down, moving her face close to Cindy-Lou's. "No, honey," she said, shaking her head. "This isn't your fault. Whoever did this didn't steal Christmas, he just stole stuff. Christmas is here." She pointed to her daughter's heart. "And no one can steal that."

Standing up, Donna offered her hand to her daughter. After a moment, Cindy-Lou took her

mother's hand. Then she offered her other hand to Groopert. He took her hand, and offered his other hand to Izzy. All the *Whos* in *Who*-ville began to join hands one by one.

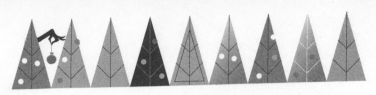

23

Up on Mt. Crumpit, the sleigh was teetering, ready to fall. The Grinch put his shoulder against the sleigh's runner. "Just one more shove," he said.

But at that moment, a faint sound floated up the mountain from *Who*-ville far below. As the sound grew louder, the Grinch strained to make sense of the noise.

"What's that?" he asked Max, cupping a hand to his ear. "Do you hear it?"

When he realized exactly what he was hearing, the Grinch was flabbergasted. "They're . . . singing!"

He was right. The sound of hundreds of happy *Whos* raising their voices to sing a Christmas carol together floated right up the mountain to the Grinch's furry green ears.

The Grinch couldn't believe it. How could they be singing a joyous song together? He'd stolen their Christmas! This was not what he'd expected! Crying and wailing? Yes! Singing? No!

"I don't understand, Max," he said.

The Grinch climbed onto the sleigh stacked with sacks of presents. Searching through the bags, he found a telescope with a bow on it. Telescope in hand, he jumped down off the sleigh and hurried over to the edge of a small rocky outcropping. He pulled the telescope open, put it to his eye, and pointed the other end at *Who*-ville.

Through the telescope, the Grinch saw all the *Whos* standing in a big circle, holding hands. Their mouths moved in perfect unison as they sang together. And they looked so . . . happy!

"Don't they know what I've done?" the Gr⁀ asked, lowering the telescope. Max shrugge⁀

The Grinch took another look,

crowd until he found Cindy-Lou *Who*. Her eyes were closed, and she smiled as she sang, lifting her face toward the sky. He heard her little voice in his head, saying, "It's so beautiful that if you close your eyes and listen, all your sadness just goes away."

Could it be true?

The Grinch lowered the telescope again. He listened carefully to the sound of the *Whos* singing together. And he felt something—something strong, deep, and profound.

Max looked at his master. What was he doing?

Closing his eyes, the Grinch tilted his head back, letting the music flow into him. He smiled. He smiled because when he listened to the music with his heart, it grew three sizes! His sadness went away! He felt a joy he'd never felt in his whole life. Bliss! And then . . .

. . . HE REALIZED THE SLEIGH WAS ABOUT TO FALL OVER THE CLIFF!

"Wha—?" he cried. "OH NO!"

As the sleigh teetered on the edge, the Grinch jumped up and grabbed the back end of the runner. 'Ie tried to stop the sleigh from falling, but it was too

heavy for him. It toppled over the edge, taking the Grinch with it! "YAAAAH!" the Grinch screamed.

Thinking quickly, the Grinch whipped out his candy cane, aimed it back up the mountain, and pressed a button. *SHWOOMP!* A grappling hook shot out the end of the candy cane and snagged the edge of the cliff. Max peered down, looking worried.

"It's okay, Max," the Grinch said. "I'm gonna—"

The rocky cliff started to crumble under the grappling hook.

"AHHH!" the Grinch shouted. "Oh, no, no, no!"

CRRRACK! The edge of the cliff broke off! The Grinch began to fall—

"MAAAAAX!" he screamed.

But then there was a tug on the rope! The Grinch looked up and saw Fred and his family pulling on the rope. Max helped, too. Working together, they pulled the Grinch and the sleigh back up to safety!

"Fred?" the Grinch said, walking toward the reindeer, amazed. "You came back!"

He looked toward *Who*-ville, full of resolve. "Come on, Max, my boy!"

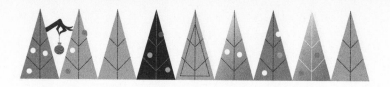

The Grinch jumped into the driver's seat. As the sleigh began to slide down the side of the mountain toward *Who*-ville, he scooped up Max and set him on the seat next to him. "ARF! ARF!" the little dog barked, wagging his tail. He was very happy to be riding instead of pulling. And the Grinch was happy to have Max with him.

As the sleigh picked up speed, the Grinch grabbed a horn, climbed onto the stack of presents, and blew it as loudly as he could to let the *Whos* know he was coming! *FA-WAAAH! FA-WOOO! FA-FA-FA-WAAAAAAH!*

The Grinch was determined to make things right. "I hope we haven't lost anyone's presents, Max," he said. The smile on Max's face said that he believed that everything would be all right.

Down in the town square, one of the *Whos* spotted the tall stack of Christmas gifts and decorations heading through town, coming right toward them! The other *Whos* turned to see the approaching tower of presents. The *Whos* stopped singing. They opened up their circle so the Grinch could slide his sleigh right into the middle.

"Uh, hello, everybody," he said awkwardly. "I've come to return your gifts. I stole your Christmas. Because . . ." He paused. Why had he stolen their Christmas, exactly? "Because I thought it would fix something that happened a long time ago."

The *Whos* looked surprised. That's not what they'd expected the mean old Grinch to say.

"But it didn't," he admitted. "And I'm sorry."

The Grinch spotted Cindy-Lou in the crowd. He walked over to her. "I'm so very sorry. For everything."

Slumping his shoulders, the Grinch turned and shuffled away, heading back toward his lonely cave. Max followed after him.

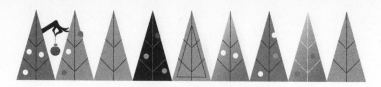

24

Once he and Max had made their way back up Mt. Crumpit, the Grinch entered his cave and headed down a hallway. Max kept following his master, but the Grinch stopped him. "Not now, Max," he said. "I need to be alone."

Max trotted off down another corridor to his bed. As he lay on the little mattress with his blanket, he stared at the framed picture of himself with his beloved master.

DING-A-LING! The bell rang, summoning Max. He sprang up from his mattress, climbed the steps,

and jumped onto the platform that pushed down into
the vat of coffee, pouring out a cup. He attached the
tray to his head and balanced the cup of hot coffee
on the tray.

But as he started to back into the little elevator
that would carry him up to the Grinch's bedroom, he
saw something.

Inside the elevator was a new ball! It had a shiny
Christmas bow on it!

"I kinda thought you might like it. If you don't
like it, I can take it back. It's not a big deal. I just
thought maybe you'd—"

"ARF! ARF!" Max barked happily. He began
playing with the ball, batting it with his paws
and then jumping on it, biting it. He loved his
new ball!

"Oh! Heh," the Grinch said, smiling. "Merry
Christmas to you, too, Max."

SQUEAK! SQUEAK! Every time Max bit the
ball, it squeaked. *SQUEAK!*

"That's gonna get old," the Grinch said, rolling
his eyes.

KNOCK! KNOCK!

"What was that?" the Grinch said, turning toward the sound. It had been so long since anyone had knocked on the cave's front door that the Grinch had forgotten what it sounded like.

KNOCK! KNOCK!

It was definitely a knock at the front door. But who could be knocking?

He made his way to the front door, opened it, and looked outside, expecting to see a furious crowd. But all he saw was Cindy-Lou *Who* standing in the snow, staring up at him with her big, round eyes.

"Uh . . . hello," the Grinch said, surprised.

"Hi!" Cindy-Lou said brightly. "Remember me?"

"Yes," the Grinch blinked as he replied. "Yes, I do. I remember you."

She stuck out her small hand. "My name is Cindy-Lou. Cindy-Lou *Who*."

"It's nice to meet you, Cindy-Lou," the Grinch said, shaking her hand. "My name is Grinch."

Down by the Grinch's feet, Max squeezed his new ball. *SQUEAK!* "And, uh, this is Max," the Grinch added.

"Whoa! Nice to meet you, Max!" Cindy-Lou

said, laughing as he licked her face. She looked back up at the Grinch. "I just came to invite you to our house for Christmas dinner."

"What?" the Grinch said. "Me? But I took your gifts!"

"Yeah," Cindy-Lou said, nodding. "I know."

"And your trees," the Grinch said.

"Yup," Cindy-Lou agreed.

"I stole your whole Christmas," he regretfully reminded her.

"I know you did," she said. "But we're inviting you anyway."

The Grinch couldn't understand why the Whos would do such a thing. "But why?" he asked, utterly bewildered.

"Because," Cindy-Lou explained, "you've been alone long enough."

She turned, walked to her sled, and started back down the mountain, calling, "Dinner's at six! Don't be late! And make sure you bring Max, too!"

The Grinch watched her go. An invitation to Christmas dinner? He'd never been invited to a Christmas dinner in his life!

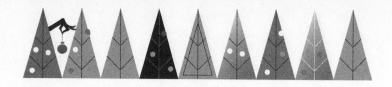

But at six o'clock that evening, the Grinch stood
outside the front door of the house where Cindy-Lou
lived with her mother and twin brothers. He wore
a black tie over his green suit. His hair was neatly
combed. Max was with him.

He was terrified.

He slowly moved his shaking finger toward the
doorbell, then yanked it back. He tried again, but
failed. "Bad idea," he muttered to himself. "I can't do
this. I can't do this!"

25

But he did. He took a deep breath and rang the bell.
DING-DONG!

"Here we go," he said to Max.

The door swung open. Donna stood in the doorway holding a big bowl with a whisk in it. "Oh, Mr. Grinch!" she said. "What a nice surprise!"

"Uh, h-hi," the Grinch stammered nervously. "I wore a tie."

Donna smiled. "It's a very nice tie." She turned and called back into the house, "Cindy-Lou, look who came to our dinner!"

Cindy-Lou ran to the front door, squeezing in beside her mom to greet the Grinch. "Mr. Grinch! You're here!" she said, excited to see him.

"Come on," she said, taking him by the hand. "I'll introduce you to everyone!"

Cindy-Lou led the Grinch through the party. Lots of *Whos* had come for dinner. One of them put her hand on the Grinch's shoulder. He whipped around, startled.

"Hello, Mr. Grinch," she said warmly. "Merry Christmas!"

"Merry Christmas to you, too," the Grinch said, surprised.

"Aunt Ida," Cindy-Lou said, "I'd like you to meet my friend the Grinch."

"It's nice to meet you, Mr. Grinch," Aunt Ida said.

"Thank you," the Grinch answered. "It's nice to be here." He smiled, beginning to feel welcome at the party.

Donna entered the room with a big tray of appetizers that smelled and looked wonderful. "Cindy-Lou? Could you make a little room for this tray?"

"I'll do that," the Grinch offered. "Let me help you." He took the tray and found a spot for it.

"Oh!" Donna said. "Thank you!"

The Grinch saw several kids playing with Max. He smiled. Then he heard a familiar voice.

"Is that grouchy, grumpy Grinchy I see standing over there?"

"Bricklebaum!" the Grinch exclaimed. "Good to see you!"

The friendly *Who* hurried over to the Grinch. "Come on, Grinchy! Give me a hug!" He grabbed the Grinch in a hearty bear hug, lifting him off the ground. "It don't count if you don't hug back, buddy!"

"Come take your seats, everyone!" Donna called from the dining room. "Dinner's ready!"

Laughing and chatting, the crowd of guests hurried into the dining room, chose seats, and sat down. Delicious smells came from the dishes on the big round table.

"Come on," Cindy-Lou said, taking the Grinch's hand again. "You're sitting next to me." She guided him to an empty chair and sat down next to him. All

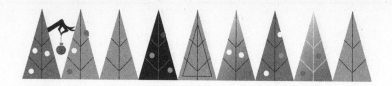

around the table, Whos were smiling and talking, ready to eat.

Under the table, Max was having a great time playing with Mabel. Bricklebaum liked to bring his dog along wherever he went. Later, he'd be sneaking little bits of food to her—and to Max, too.

Everyone seemed completely relaxed. Everyone, that is, except the Grinch, who still felt a good bit uncomfortable in these unfamiliar surroundings. "This is my first Christmas dinner," he confided to Cindy-Lou. "What happens?"

"You'll see," Cindy-Lou assured him.

Through the door from the kitchen came Donna carrying a big platter with a beautiful Roast Beast on it. The Grinch watched as she stopped and set the platter down right in front of him.

"Would you do the honors, please, Mr. Grinch?"

"Me?" he asked, amazed.

Donna nodded, smiling.

"Okay," he agreed. He reached for the big carving knife and fork. But before he started, he pushed back his chair and stood up. "Do you mind if I say something first?"

"Not at all," Donna said.

"Well," the Grinch began, "Um, well, everybody, I just want to say I've spent my entire life hating Christmas and everything about it."

The *Whos* stared at him. What was the Grinch going to say next?

"But now," he continued, "I see it wasn't Christmas that I hated. It was being alone." He took a breath and stood up a little straighter. "But I'm not alone anymore." He looked out at everyone seated around the big table and smiled. "And I have all of you to thank for it." Then he turned to Cindy-Lou, sitting in the chair next to his, looking up at him. "And especially this little girl right here." He turned to Donna. "Ma'am, your daughter's kindness changed my life."

Donna hugged Cindy-Lou. "That's my girl," she said.

"Oh, that was beautiful," Bricklebaum said, brushing away a tear. He turned to the *Who* seated next to him and whispered, "That's my best friend."

"Merry Christmas, Mr. Grinch," Cindy-Lou said, smiling widely.

"Merry Christmas, Cindy-Lou," the Grinch said.

The Grinch raised his glass, his heart full of good cheer. Everyone around the table raised theirs, too, joining him in a Christmas toast.

"To kindness and love," he said, "the things we need most."

And with that, the Grinch began to serve the slices of Roast Beast to his friends.